QUEST FOR THE
HISTORICAL ARTHUR

Quest for the Historical Arthur

A Kalamazoo Story

TIGGY MCLAUGHLIN

Cover art by Dean Ferraro

First Printing, 2021

For Terry the Barbarian and Justin II

PREFACE

This is a work of fiction. There are no real people in this story. All characters are products of my imagination. If you know me in real life and think you see yourself in one of the characters, you may be correct, but that character is not "you." Rather, you may have been the inspiration for one aspect of that particular character. (And you may also have inspired another aspect of a different character!) If you don't know me in real life, any resemblance you may have to a character is coincidental.

I wrote this novel just for fun in the fall of 2017 when I was pregnant with a spring baby and knew I would miss Kalamazoo in 2018 to stay home with him. I made substantial revisions after returning to Kalamazoo in 2019. I produced the final draft, which you are reading, in the winter of 2021 while the COVID-19 pandemic has continued to prevent in-person academic conferences. The announcement that Kalamazoo will hold a virtual conference in 2022 as well inspired me to share this novel with others who, like me, spend some of their lives at conferences and are missing that interaction right now. It is my hope that some of you can "go to Kalamazoo" this year by following Annie on her adventures there, or at least get a chuckle at reading about some in-person Kalamazoo experiences that we may one day share again.

I would first of all like to thank my medievalist friends, those who I met at Kalamazoo and those I met elsewhere but now only see at Kalamazoo, for being the inspiration behind this novel. I also want to thank all my writing buddies from NaNoWriMo and my non-writing friends who cheer me on every November I undertake to write a first draft. I am grateful to Ray for teaching me the craft of (re)writing, to Dean for his cover and character designs - they capture the tone of the novel perfectly, to Alice for promoting this work, and to Jonathan for encouraging me to publish one of the novels I always seem to be writing. I finally did it.

I bear full responsibility for any shortcomings or oversights in this novel, and recognize that they are a function of my own limited perspective. I offer my apologies to scholars of Arthurian studies, post-Roman Britain, and ancient Celtic and Roman magic: the Arthurian aspect of my novel is purely fantasy. At the end of the day, my writer self took the reins from my historian self and pursued the plot. I hope you enjoy the ride. Kalamazoo awaits.

CONTENTS

| 1 |

Memory

Wales, 537

Sunrise was still hours away when Mordred awoke. Without making a sound, he threw on his cloak and shoes and headed outside. He found his horse tied up in the meager stable next to the cottage where he'd spent the night. She was still saddled. Mordred got on and started to ride, ignoring the mare's cries of protest. He didn't have time to see to her needs.

The rest of the town was still asleep. Once outside the walls, though, Mordred could hear shouts in the distance. Somewhere off to his left, he thought he saw some light flash orange. Could the fires still be burning? He steered his horse in the other direction. He needed to get as far away from Camlann as possible.

Mordred blinked a few times and shook his head. He could put a lot of miles between himself and the ravaged land where he had fought with Arthur, his uncle. (And father? Mordred was still trying to conceive of this possibility.) But there was no way to escape what he had been through. Just thinking about the previous night brought his heart rate up, and suddenly he was back in the midst of battle. He could hear the cries and smell the destruction. He saw the man he thought he knew and the monster he knew he had to destroy. And finally, the feeling of utter defeat welled up within him, all over again.

He hadn't had time to process the events of the night before, not in his two hours of dreamless sleep, which he was now beginning to realize was more of a faint. His mind had not had time to create the narrative that would become his memory of that day. He wouldn't let it. If he had his way, no one would remember his fight at Camlann at all. No one would remember Mordred's defeat. No one would remember King Arthur and his *heroic* reign.

Mordred spat. Arthur kept returning to the forefront of his thoughts. He forced himself to look out on the horizon and see what was up ahead of him instead of what was already in his past. The sky was starting to turn gray. People would be waking soon. That was all right. He was nearing his destination.

Smoke appeared over the trees in the distance and Mordred breathed a sigh of relief, knowing that the smoke came from the witch's chimney. Good, he thought, she was at home. And awake. He shifted the pack he carried with him to the front of his body, between his knees. As if the small, worn-out brown sack were in any danger of being stolen.

He entered the forest and slowed his horse to a trot, and finally a walk, as he reached the dwelling. A silent approach was not necessary, though. The witch had powers Mordred did not understand. She was waiting for him on her doorstep wearing a shimmering green gown that matched the forest, and a seductive smile.

For a moment, Mordred considered turning around. Going back to Merlin or heading east into oblivion. Anything to avoid having to ask the witch for help. Arthur's face resurfaced in Mordred's mind once again — this time grimacing in agony as Mordred slid his sword between two ribs. Arthur would die a hero. Mordred wondered whether the witch had put that image into his mind. He clutched his pack close to his body and started to dismount.

"You're alive," Morgan said, by way of greeting. She sounded bemused.

Mordred realized he was feeling the same way she sounded. He had no idea how he was still alive, much less able to ride a horse mere hours after he thought he was going to die from his wounds. His face contorted in pain as he dismounted, the motion reminding him of the hole near his hip. It wasn't bleeding anymore, thanks to the treatment of Merlin and his servant girl.

Morgan chuckled. "You need my help."

Mordred turned and forced himself to face the witch. He despised the way her face looked. It was so beautiful — more beautiful than any face he had ever laid eyes on — and he hated that someone so evil should have such a pleasing face. She was smiling, the ends of her thin mouth turned up ever so slightly, matching the creases in the corners of her sparkling emerald eyes. Morgan knew she was beautiful, and Mordred hated that, too.

"Come inside and let me have a look at that codex."

Mordred stopped cold and clutched his bag closer to him, reaching in to make sure the folded piece of parchment was still safe inside. He swallowed. "Thank you, milady," he made himself say before following her into her tiny house without a backward glance at the horse he was sure he would never see again.

The inside of the house was dark, lit only by the small fire burning under a cauldron in the center of the room. Mordred felt his confidence increase now that he could no longer see Morgan so clearly. He gravitated toward the fire, not realizing how cold he was until he felt the warmth. "I need assistance with a curse," he said shortly.

"Show me the codex," Morgan said. She wasn't talking to Mordred. She was talking to his bag, which floated over to her and emptied itself onto her lap. Mordred took a deep breath. There was no turning back now.

Morgan lifted the parchment into her delicate fingers, smiling with all her teeth, and spoke slowly, "You want to destroy Arthur's memory." When she said it like that, it sounded far more sinister than what Mordred actually had in mind. He simply wanted people's memory of Arthur to fade, for him not to go down in history as some hero, some legend. "You want people to remember Arthur as a villain," she said. "As he really is. How fascinating."

No, *no*, Mordred thought with all his might. But when he opened his mouth, he only said, "I've already prepared the spell. I just need your magic."

"Of course, of course." Morgan stroked the parchment with one long fingernail. She was already getting started, Mordred realized. She continued to speak as she stroked, without taking her eyes off the codex. "These pages will contain the true memory of Arthur. Once they enter into the world and someone unknown to Arthur reads these words aloud, all will remember him as who he truly was — a coward, a murderer — nay — a slayer of nations."

Mordred gasped. Was that who Arthur truly was?

"I will need to make a sacrifice," Morgan continued. Mordred nodded. He had anticipated there would be a price. "Your horse is sickly, but she will do."

"Of course, milady," Mordred answered, still nodding his head.

Morgan clapped her hands. "Good," she said. "I shall perform the spell straightaway. There is just one thing," she added, suddenly snapping up her neck and fixing Mordred with a lethal stare. Her eyes were black. Mordred could have sworn they were green when he first arrived. "You must not show the codex to Merlin."

"W-why not?" Mordred asked, caught off guard.

"Merlin has other power," Morgan replied vaguely. "If the spell is completed before Merlin touches these pages, then his magic cannot breach it. But if he gets his hands on this codex before a stranger can read the words —" She trailed off. "His power is great," she whispered. That was all she said.

Mordred gulped and took a step backward, almost falling into the cauldron. Merlin had done more than touch the folded piece of parchment. He had given it to Mordred. It was Merlin who had plucked Mordred from the battlefield right when he thought he was going to die. It was Merlin who brought him to his house on the edge of the forest and healed his wounds. It was Merlin who helped him prepare the spell, initially. It was only when Mordred realized that Merlin guessed what he intended to do with the codex that Mordred decided to seek out Morgan. He could not tell her that the damage was already done.

"I promise," Mordred choked. "Merlin will not see these pages. Thank you for your help."

Morgan scowled and went back to stroking the parchment.

Mordred would have to hide the codex, far away from Merlin. Eventually, someone unknown to Arthur would find it and read the words and complete the spell. He hoped.

But Merlin's power was so great, even Morgan would not speak of it.

| 2 |

The New, New Manuscript

Michigan, 2017

Annie walked out of the conference room into a burst of confetti.

"Congratulations, PhD candidate!" Annie's roommate Gina shouted from behind the confetti. She shoved a balloon in Annie's face. "How'd it go? You are a candidate, right?"

"Jesus, Gina, you scared me!" Annie clutched at her heart and stood up against the wall.

"She did well, and yes, she is a candidate now." Annie's supervisor Murray Penge, a tall, thin older man who used a ski pole as a cane answered Gina's question as he filed out of the conference room behind two women who were also on Annie's exam committee. "And I'm glad to see you have such an enthusiastic supporter."

Gina beamed as Annie shrank against the wall.

"While you no doubt have plans to celebrate with your friends, do you mind very much meeting with me to discuss your exam first?" Murray asked Annie.

"No, of course not!" Annie's voice was high. She had known Murray for three years and sometimes still interacted with him like he was the biggest deal in early medieval history and she was just an amateurish fangirl. Murray Penge actually was an important and well-known medieval historian, but he was also Annie's advisor and the man who was supposed to direct her dissertation writing for the next three years, and though Annie was a fan of his work, she was by no means amateurish.

"Let's go to my office." He turned to Gina and added, "I won't keep your friend long."

"Can you text Amy I'll be about a half hour late?" Annie muttered to her roommate.

Gina smiled broadly. "I'll do you one better — I'll head to the Blue Leprechaun now and hold down the fort until you arrive."

Annie smiled back and followed Murray down the hall toward his office. She could always count on Gina to enjoy herself, even if she was about to be the only scientist at a table full of historians.

Inside Murray's office, Annie sat down in one of the two cheap classroom chairs that were the only furniture in the room except for a half-filled metal bookshelf and a simple brown table that held nothing except for a shabby MacBook. Murray's office had grown sparser and sparser since Annie's first meeting with him when she just started graduate school. He planned on retiring soon, but would stay long enough to advise Annie's dissertation. At that first meeting, the room had been filled with books — piles and piles of books on the table, under the table, and all along a credenza that was no longer in the room. Now Murray's only personal belongings consisted of three shelves' worth of books on the bookcase and the MacBook.

Murray smiled. "I know, I know," he said, anticipating the question in Annie's eyes. "I've moved a lot of my things out already. Given away a lot of books — as you know!" As his last student, Annie was the lucky recipient of several of Murray's books, including some expensive volumes that she wouldn't own otherwise.

Annie smiled as she recalled the first book Murray had given her on their very first meeting. It was a 15th-century incunable that bore the title "Mediaeval Grimoire Containing the Spelles of Morgana le Fey." Annie's eyes had gravitated to that book the second she entered Murray's office, and it was for that reason that he decided to give it to her.

"Congratulations, you passed the test," he had said in his too-quiet voice. "You instantly detected the oldest object in the room. That's how I can tell you're a real historian."

Annie still felt a little embarrassed about that encounter, even though it was ages ago and the grimoire had sat untouched on her bookshelf for the better part of the last two years. She was certain that Murray didn't remember how awkward she had been at their first meeting. He had just finished praising her for how she performed on her oral exam. And he had given away enough books over the past three years that he was unlikely to recall the exact circumstances of each gift.

"What did you think of our discussion today?" he asked. He was referring to the exam. Murray always talked about monumental events as if they were a casual walk to the corner for coffee. Annie supposed that when you're as big a deal as Murray was, things like prelim exams for graduate students really did seem like a coffee break.

"I think it went well," Annie started, trying to pull her mind away from the grimoire at home on her bookshelf. "I could answer everyone's questions. Nothing surprised me."

"That is more than most people can say about their oral exam. It shows you had a good written exam."

Annie felt her cheeks flush and immediately wondered why. She *had* written a very good exam. She had worked so hard all year reading just about every work on early medieval saints and nuns she could get her hands on and finally felt like she had a firm grasp on her field and was ready to contribute to it. "I felt like I was prepared."

Murray smiled. "I'll say you were. Do you feel prepared to write a dissertation?"

Yes, Annie thought, she did. She had never felt more prepared for anything in her entire life. She nodded.

Murray nodded back. "Once again, you are ahead of most people at this stage in the PhD process. A good many don't ever feel ready to write their dissertation, even after they've written it!"

Annie nodded again. She needed to say something. "I feel ready. I already know how I want it to start. I could even start writing it right now." That was too much.

"Don't do that!" Murray exclaimed, with more emotion than he normally injected into his words. Annie was startled. "You need to give yourself a break."

"Oh, it's fine. I manage my time well," she answered. This was true. Annie prided herself on her work-life balance. She did not like to admit that work-life balance was extremely easy to achieve as a single person who had forsworn dating, at least for the time being, but preferred to focus on the very fact of its achievement. She got all her work done and had a healthy diet and got enough sleep. Talking to her fellow graduate students, she knew that was a real accomplishment.

"I'm not talking about that kind of break," said Murray, "although I'm glad to hear that you have healthy habits. I mean you need to give your mind a break. You need to step away from the early middle ages for a little bit, so that when you approach the period again you will have fresh eyes for starting a dissertation."

Annie frowned. She did not like being told to stop doing work.

Murray answered her frown with a smile and continued, "Go out with your friends, to the Blue Leprechaun. Don't read anything tonight. Or for a week. Then, when you do feel like reading something, pick up something from outside of your field, just to exercise your brain without feeling the sense of urgency that you will feel once you decide you are doing research for your dissertation. Just grab something off your shelf. Maybe that old grimoire I gave you when we first met."

Annie looked up, her mouth open. "What?"

"Do you think I wouldn't remember our first meeting?"

"No, of course not," Annie said, shaking her head. Of course the mention was a coincidence. Murray couldn't have known she was just thinking about it. But now Annie was even more eager to go home and check on the grimoire. Something about it had never felt right to her from the very beginning, which was one of the main reasons why it had sat on a book shelf for the past two years. The other reason was Marshall, an acquaintance she once had who had been very interested in the grimoire, and whom Annie would rather not think about. She looked down at her phone to check the time.

"Go on, go on," Murray said. "I don't want you to keep your friends waiting. I just wanted to congratulate you, and to tell you to rest."

"Thanks Murray," said Annie.

"Send me an email in a month" he said. "Then we can talk about your dissertation."

Annie took Murray's advice and rested from work. She didn't read a single word of academic prose for four whole days, which had to be some kind of record for her. She didn't even open the grimoire, although it tempted her a few times. When she returned home from the bar the night of her exam, she saw it on the shelf and for a fleeting instant thought she should open it to see if there was anything in there that Murray might have been alluding to at their meeting. Then she realized that entire chain of thoughts was absurd, and promptly went to bed and slept for twelve hours. Murray was more right about Annie needing a break than even he knew.

Four days later, though, she was ready to get back to work. She spent the morning at the library paging through references, requesting books, and diving down bibliographical rabbit holes with a euphoria she hadn't felt since she began her undergrad thesis. When she got back to her apartment at lunch time, she was actually whistling.

"You're awful cheery today," Gina commented from the kitchen table where she sat with her laptop open to some news site, a sandwich on a paper towel on the keyboard.

"Just started my dissertation," Annie said, setting down her bag and pouring herself a glass of iced green tea. "Sort of. I went to the library."

Gina giggled and muttered, "Humanities," as she got up to get her own glass of tea. "Hey, I wanted to tell you, I won't be able to go to dinner Friday night. Ed's parents decided they were going to visit this weekend and I have to go with them."

Annie shrugged. "That's okay," she said. "We can go next weekend."

"And we'll still go to dinner all the time when I live with Ed," Gina added, reading Annie's mind. "Until you realize that your new roommate is much cooler than I am and you would rather hang out with her."

"Or until I get a boyfriend and need to have dinner with his parents all the time," said Annie sardonically.

Gina almost spit out her tea. "What? You're dating?" she exclaimed. "Dating, and you didn't even tell me? Is this because you passed your prelims?"

Annie wished she hadn't made the joke. She was not dating, and didn't plan on starting any time soon. She was still recovering from the unhealthy relationship she had been in for all four years of college. When she got to grad school she decided that she was not going to date for awhile and focus on herself. The experience was liberating, and every day she felt more and more grateful to have only herself to answer to. To top it all off, her studies and progress to degree could not have been going more smoothly without the distraction of romance, and she did not feel ready to give all that up just yet.

"No, I'm not dating," was all she said.

"Oh boo." Gina sat back down at her laptop. "Well you'll tell me when you do though, right?"

"Of course I will." Annie took a seat at the table and glanced over at Gina's laptop screen, surprised to see someone she recognized.

The screen actually showed the University of Michigan home-page, and the cover story featured an English professor Annie recognized from the monthly Medieval Lunches the different departments hosted. The headline read, "Arthurian Scholar Finds New Manuscript."

"What's that?" Annie asked.

"Oh yeah, I was going to show you this," said Gina. "Some medievalist here just found a new manuscript about King Arthur. Do you know her?"

Annie couldn't believe what she was hearing, all thoughts of dating and relationships immediately gone from her mind. "A *new* new manuscript?" she asked.

"Is there such a thing as an old new manuscript?" asked Gina, puzzled.

"Well sometimes someone finds a thing that's been found before but they didn't read the publication, or it wasn't published —"

Gina clicked on the link and started reading out loud: "'Betty Randall, professor of English and Women's Studies, had an interesting trip to the archives this summer.' Okay, blah blah, 'she announced this Thursday —'"

"Give me that!" Annie turned Gina's laptop to face her and started scanning the text quickly, her mouth hanging open.

After a moment, Gina spoke. "So I'm guessing she *did* find a new, new manuscript?"

Annie nodded and kept reading. When she got to the end of the article, she said, "Apparently Betty Randall unearthed an unknown manuscript in some obscure church in England over the summer. She spent months trying to authenticate it, and tracking down previous publications." Annie glanced over at Gina at this point with a look that said, "See?"

"And?"

"And she couldn't find any. Apparently this really is a new, new manuscript."

"Well that's exciting, right?" asked Gina, jumping up from her chair. "Aren't you excited? In my field, whenever somebody does something new, which, granted, is all the time, because it's biology, but anyway, we all get really excited and celebrate and stuff! Aren't you going to find this person and go celebrate? Isn't she having a thing here in the English department that you can go attend because you're a medievalist too?"

"I don't know. If there is, I haven't heard anything about it," said Annie. "But it says here she's presenting it at the big medieval studies conference in Kalamazoo next month. Maybe I should go to that." Annie had been toying with the idea of going to Kalamazoo for months now. She had never been to a big conference before and was unbelievably intimidated, but now that she was a candidate she supposed it was time to just bite the bullet and go.

"Oh yeah, you should *totally* go to the conference," said Gina. "But you should track this lady down, too. Isn't her office in the same building as yours?"

"Well yeah, but English is a completely different department from history. I've only ever been up there two times, for the two Medieval Lunches that met in the English seminar room. I don't know any of those people. It would be weird for me to just knock on her door and say, 'Hey, I saw an article about you on *the university website*, along with *the rest of the world.*'"

"Didn't you used to be friends with an English grad student?"

Whoa, Gina had a good memory. "You mean Marshall?" Annie asked, feeling a sudden chill at the memory of a friend she had almost made her first year.

Marshall had been a third year when Annie met him at her first Medieval Lunch. Initially, she felt comfortable with him, which was a rarity for Annie and single men. Marshall had seemed much more interested in Annie's grimoire than Annie herself, however, which put her at ease knowing that she wasn't about to be entangled in a flirtation.

At first, the two had bonded over their common interest in Arthurian legend, and Annie agreed to look through the spells of Morgan le Fay with him. But when he got his hands on the book, Marshall only wanted to look at one spell — the strange spell in the center of the volume that looked nothing like the rest of the spells. It even looked like it was written on a different type of parchment. Marshall had been fascinated by the gibberish script that the spell surrounded. "The lost sigils of King Arthur," he had called them. Annie had translated the spell from the Latin — a feat that made Marshall entirely too excited for Annie's comfort — and then she and Marshall had nothing left to talk about. They saw each other around now and then after that, but it was awkward and after awhile they stopped saying hi to each other at Medieval Lunches.

"Marshall was a creeper," Annie said to Gina. "He used me to translate part of *my* grimoire for him. I haven't talked to him since my first year. I don't even think I've seen him around at all recently. He might be away doing research this year."

Gina frowned. "Hmm. I still don't think it would be super weird for you to go talk to this professor on your own, though. Sure, you read the article on a public forum where everyone else in the world could have seen it too, but you're not everyone else in the world. You're a grad student at this very institution studying basically the same thing, just in a different department."

"Not 'basically the same thing'," Annie replied. She was now reading Betty Randall's bio on the university website. "Randall mostly studies Welsh poetry. Which, to be fair, a lot of Arthurian legend is Welsh poetry, but she doesn't do historical study of post-Roman Britain. And I don't know nearly as much about Britain in this time period as I probably should."

Gina waved her head back and forth. "That might be the case," she said in her sing-song voice, "but just so you know, you're not a total rando."

Annie sighed. "I know I'm not." But Annie didn't quite believe herself. "I'll see her at Kalamazoo. I should probably go to that conference anyway. It's only a ninety minute drive away. I don't really have an excuse not to go."

"And now," Gina said, gesturing wildly at her laptop screen, "you have an excuse *to* go."

| 3 |

The Lost Sigils of King Arthur

She probably would see Marshall at Kalamazoo, Annie realized when she turned in for the night. She had been thinking about the conference all day — how she was going to ask Betty Randall a really astute question at the end of her paper and then introduce herself to her when the session was over. In her mind she was surrounded by other history graduate students when she approached the professor, even though all of her history friends were modernists and would not be attending Kalamazoo. More likely, she would be standing next to Marshall.

She pulled the old grimoire off her shelf for the first time in ages and actually laughed out loud as she finally admitted to herself that Marshall would *definitely* be at Betty Randall's paper. He was obsessed with King Arthur. There was no way he wasn't going to be at a paper on a brand new Arthurian manuscript. As a matter of fact, he was probably sitting outside of Betty Randall's office right now, waiting to hold the door open for her so she could tell him more about the manuscript. Annie shuddered.

She opened the grimoire to the center fold that contained the spell she had translated for Marshall and felt a different sort of chill.

This chill had nothing to do with her memories of Marshall. Annie had felt this exact chill the first time she touched those pages in Murray's office, the first time she ever held the book. The parchment of these center pages was a different color from the rest, and it even felt different. The pages also looked different. Most pages featured an ornately calligraphed spell title and a woodblock print image above two columns of text indicating a description of the spell and instructions on how to perform it. This page had no such images, but instead featured an intricate knot of what looked like capital letters on each side. The Lost Sigils of King Arthur. Marshall had said they were supposed to be Arthur's personal insignia or something. Surrounding the sigils was some faded Latin script that Marshall had transcribed and Annie had translated.

There was no question that these pages were not originally part of the book. Annie could sense it as well as deduce it from their physical characteristics. Marshall could sense it too, and he had made no secret of the fact that he was only interested in these pages and the mysterious "sigils" they contained. Annie had never heard of the Lost Sigils of King Arthur, but Marshall had said he was part of some online community devoted to discovering the lost sigils and he couldn't believe he just discovered them himself in Annie's book. Annie never bothered to check whether his online community existed. It was probably some site for conspiracy theorists or something. The whole thing sounded seriously ahistorical. But Marshall had been happy with Annie's translation. Too happy, as Annie recalled.

Stuck in the fold of the parchment was the piece of notebook paper where Annie had written the translation that day in the library. Marshall could decipher the text on his own, but he had needed Annie to translate the words. "*Memoriam Arturi contemnamus; non heros, sed homicida; mille gentes occidebat saevus Arturius; non Mordredus conservare potest,*" the paper read in Marshall's stilted handwriting. Then below it, in Annie's cursive, "Let us scorn the memory of Arthur. He was not a hero, but a murderer. Cruel Arthur killed a thousand nations. Mordred could not save them."

Annie shivered again as memories of that night came flooding back to her. How Marshall had asked her to read the words aloud in Latin, and then in English, and again in Latin. The same strange feeling she got when her hands touched the parchment passed through her when she read the Latin words, and for a brief moment she felt as if she had performed a magic spell. After she left the library and was no longer with Marshall, she realized that that thought was ridiculous. Even if those words were a real spell at one time, her reading them did not mean she performed magic.

But as she sat alone in her room two years later, reading over her translation in light of the new manuscript discovery, Annie couldn't help but think that maybe the manuscript was going to change the historical memory of King Arthur. She had to talk to Betty Randall.

Annie did her best to put Marshall out of her mind over the next few weeks as she planned for Kalamazoo. The semester was over, Murray did not want to hear from her before the end of the month, and she told herself that the biggest thing she had to worry about was what to wear to her first conference. For that, she needed help.

Even as Gina's long-term roommate, Annie had never expected to find herself sitting on her bed in front of an empty suitcase while Gina went through her closet judging every article of clothing she owned. She had managed to avoid dating, but didn't realize that making her debut in the world of academia was going to be just as stressful, and involve just as much curating of one's physical appearance to impress complete strangers.

Annie looked out the window. It was early May, and already all of the undergrads were gone. Ann Arbor seemed like an entirely different town. Annie loved Ann Arbor in May and June — after the majority of students left but before the tourists and hot weather arrived. She turned back to Gina, who still had her back to her as she rifled through Annie's clothes using increasingly angry strokes.

"Okay, well I suppose you won't need a suit, since you're not presenting," said Gina, "but don't you have a blazer?"

"I have one blazer," Annie replied, getting up. "I think it's in the back there somewhere."

Gina dug and pulled out a bright purple blazer with a cinched waist. "Purple? A little bold, no?" Gina asked.

"I don't know. I never wore it."

Gina hung it back up. "Come on. I have a navy blazer that should fit you. You could probably wear it two days — once with a skirt and once with a pair of pants. And, how many days are you going?"

"Three," said Annie. "But really it's two. I'll get there Thursday night so I won't need to wear anything special that day. Then there's Friday and Saturday, and I'll probably come home Saturday night unless I somehow make friends there and want to stay for the dance."

"There's a dance?" Gina exclaimed. "Stay where you are!" She ran into her room. Annie flopped back down onto the bed, trying to imagine what skirt or pants she owned that could possibly match Gina's preppy blazer.

Gina returned two seconds later, brandishing the blazer and four different dresses. "Okay," she said, laying the clothes onto Annie's bed with a flourish. "This blazer will match anything, including all your graphic tees. The J. Crew models are always putting graphic tees under blazers," she added with mixed bemusement and disapproval. She folded the jacket in half and placed it gently into Annie's suitcase. "Now, these dresses are all different, so I want you to try them all on and choose the one that most fits your style."

"Do I have to?"

"You could just pack them all and try them on there," Gina replied, sounding somewhat disappointed. "But then you'll have to call me and tell you how you look in them." She smiled and batted her eyelashes. "I would say send pics, but I know you wouldn't do that."

Annie rolled her eyes. "Fine. Let's pack the rest of the clothes first, though, since I do have to go to the rest of the conference, but I haven't actually committed to the dance yet."

"Fair enough." Gina returned to Annie's closet. "You can probably wear your skinny jeans and a t-shirt with the blazer one day, if not two, but you'll need something a little dressier for the day you go to that professor's talk. How about this?" She pulled out a gray pencil skirt that was at least ten years old and held it up. Annie wrinkled her nose. "Pencil skirts are back in," Gina assured her. "Try it on — see how it looks. You can wear a tank top with it under the blazer. Then, for the last day…" Gina disappeared back into the closet and emerged with an orange wool sweater. "This! PS — I love this. Why don't you wear this all the time?"

Annie shrugged. "I forgot I had it."

Gina packed the sweater in Annie's suitcase before Annie could object. "Why didn't we do this sooner?" Gina asked. "We're going to have to have a closet date slash shopping spree before I move. Promise me you'll remind me if I forget?"

"I will," Annie replied without quite making eye contact.

"Liar," said Gina. "Don't worry — I won't forget."

"Speaking of," said Annie, getting back up and grabbing the grimoire off her bookshelf, "I don't want to forget this."

"What are you doing?" Gina asked. "We still need to pick out the rest of your clothes! What about heels?"

"I'm not wearing heels," Annie said dismissively. "The Western Michigan campus is ginormous and by the looks of this program, I'll be walking all over it. I'm wearing my Doc Martens, and that's it."

"Well at least take one pair of dress shoes for the dance. You might need to repack everything into a bigger suitcase if you're bringing that huge book. Here, I'll get mine—"

"No, I'm not bringing the book," Annie said. "I'm just taking photos of the relevant pages." She got out her phone and started photographing all around the cover of the book before opening it up to the center spread. She didn't care about the rest of the book, but if that new manuscript did contain some information that defamed King Arthur, Annie wanted to show these pages to Betty Randall. She also photographed the notebook paper with her translation.

"What are those pages?" asked Gina, leaning over Annie's shoulder.

"I'm not really sure," said Annie, "but I'm curious if it relates to the new Arthur manuscript. I plan on taking all these photos to Professor Randall after her talk on Saturday. Maybe some of the other people presenting at that session or attending it know something about them. I figure it would be a good idea to get a bunch of Arthurian scholars in the same room together, and then show them this."

Gina nodded. "Yes, that does sound like a good plan."

"Can you just do me a big favor while I'm gone?"

"Of course — anything! Water your jade plant?"

"No, that won't need watered in the next few days. Just watch over this book." Annie hefted the grimoire back into its spot on the bookshelf. "It'll be right here. But just make sure nothing happens to it. Don't let anyone in my room. And if anyone, um, randomly asks about it, just tell them I brought it to Kalamazoo with me, and don't let them in."

Gina raised an eyebrow. "Do you think anything like that's going to happen?"

"I don't know." Annie shrugged, considering it. "Probably not. I just get this feeling, though. I'm a little uneasy about the whole thing."

"I'll watch your book for you. And if you need anything — if anything makes you uneasy at the conference — promise you'll call me?"

"Nothing's going to happen at the conference."

"But if something does. Please, Annie?"

"All right." Annie smiled. "Thanks, Gina."

| 4 |

Kalamazoo

It rained all the way to Kalamazoo, and the weather showed no signs of letting up when Annie pulled into the crowded parking lot around Valley Three, one of the three Western Michigan University dormitories that housed the conference goers for the weekend. Annie was glad she was wearing her skinny jeans and Doc Martens instead of some less rain-worthy combination Gina had tried to push on her. But she did put on Gina's blazer over her Death Cab for Cutie t-shirt before she went inside the dorm to register.

The inside of Valley Three was even more chaotic than the parking lot. The lobby was full of medievalists of all ages, including some monks and nuns in full habit, all running in every direction, looking down at their phones, talking on their phones, and otherwise trying any way they could to coordinate meetings with colleagues they hadn't seen since last year. Aside from the clergy, Annie noticed, everyone was wearing different colors and styles of clothing. No one seemed to agree upon what professional conference attire looked like. The only thing they had in common was that every single one of them wore a card around their neck, advertising their name, pronouns, and institution in bold, black letters.

Along the back and right walls of the room were folding tables staffed by undergraduates in bright pink t-shirts. Catching sight of them, Annie pushed her way to the nearest registration table, where a student said, "Last name?"

"Fisher," Annie replied.

The student pointed at a table on the other side of the room bearing a sign that said A-F. Annie sighed and hefted her suitcase back through the crowd.

"Fisher," she said, a little out of breath, when she got to the A-F table.

"Annie? You're in Valley One." The student handed her a cheap lanyard and a huge manila folder. "Name card's inside your folder," he recited blankly. "There's also an envelope in here with your key and your room number on it. There's a fifty dollar replacement fee if you lose the key, so don't put it in your name tag."

"Thanks." Annie bent down to lift her suitcase again, and the student gave a pitying sigh. "If you have a car, you might want to drive up the hill to Valley One. There's more parking up there, too."

"Thanks," Annie said again. Without looking back, she pushed her way as quickly as she could through the Valley Three vestibule and parking lot and tried not to look embarrassed as she shoved her suitcase back into the trunk of her car.

Valley One looked exactly the same as Valley Three — a clinical, cinder-block dorm of 1960s vintage. The only difference was that Valley One was empty. While Valley Three had been a bustling crossroads of what seemed like ten different conferences all converging on one another, Valley One felt like exactly what it was: a tired college dormitory. That made it extra depressing. Annie was okay with the lack of activity in Valley One, though. At least it was quiet. She got in the elevator alone and wandered down the empty third-floor hallway to her bedroom.

The room itself wasn't any worse than the dorm she had lived in when she was a college freshman. It was sparse, but when you came right down to it, it had everything a dormitory really needed. Two beds, two desks, two dressers, and a trash can all sat on a shiny tile floor. In fact, this room was arguably a little better than Annie's freshman dorm because it had a bathroom that connected to one other dorm room on the other side, which was definitely preferable to having to shower down the hall.

On one of the beds sat a pile of things the conference organizers deemed appropriate amenities. Annie had to admit these were a little meager, consisting only of a towel and two wash cloths, stiff with bleach, a top sheet, a flattened pillow, and the saddest blanket she had ever seen. Annie made a mental note to bring a sleeping bag and pillow next time she came to Kalamazoo. If there was a next time. Finally, on top of the dresser she noticed a bar of soap in a wrapper and two plastic cups, also in wrappers. Not much, but enough to survive in a dorm for the weekend.

Annie plopped down on a bed and opened her conference program. It felt like a paperback novel in her hands. She couldn't believe how big this conference was, and yet she probably didn't know a soul there. She started to laugh as she realized how ridiculous she must be, to come to this massive conference without having any plans except to attend one session. According to the program, Betty Randall's session on "Arthuriana" took place the following afternoon at 1:30pm in a building called Bernhard. Annie did the math and determined that, assuming she got a full night's sleep that night, she would have approximately ten hours to find out where Bernhard was. She was also going to have to eat three full meals before then. She looked down at her watch. It was a little past five. Resigning herself to the fact that she would actually have to encounter people if she wanted to eat dinner, she took a deep breath and left the dorm room, leaving her suitcase still packed in the middle of the floor.

There were a few people milling about in the Valley One lobby when Annie got downstairs. She did not expect to know anyone, though, and was surprised when someone called her name.

"Annie Fisher!" came a vaguely familiar voice from behind her. "Is this your first Kalamazoo?"

Annie turned around and came face to face with the last person she wanted to talk to, but found herself smiling anyway at the sight of someone she knew. "Oh, hi Marshall," she said, trying her hardest to sound emotionless. "Yeah, this is my first Kalamazoo."

"Going down to the wine hour?" Marshall asked. He was grinning and friendly again, just like when they first met, which seemed strange to Annie seeing as they hadn't spoken to each other in two years.

"Wine hour?"

"Yep. Everyone meets in the Valley Three courtyards for wine while they find the people they're supposed to go to dinner with. I'm heading down there now — come on!"

"All right," Annie heard herself say before she had a chance to think. Marshall grinned again and started to walk toward the door, and Annie had no choice but to follow. She took a few deep breaths and fell into step beside Marshall. She pushed aside the resentment she had toward Marshall for his two-year-old offense, and her feeling of discomfort at walking alone with a guy. There were thousands of people at Kalamazoo. If Marshall got creepy, all she had to do was disappear into the crowd. Besides, he could be useful. He seemed to know the conference pretty well. Maybe he could tell her where the best place was to have dinner by yourself without attracting too much attention.

"So what papers have you seen so far?" he asked in his friendly-sounding voice.

"I haven't been to any yet," Annie replied. "I really only came for the 'Arthuriana' session tomorrow afternoon."

"Is that the one with Betty?"

Annie nodded. "You know her?"

"Of course I know her — she's my advisor!" Suddenly Annie felt more than a little stupid for being afraid to see Betty while they were still in Ann Arbor. Every eminent scholar at the university was also somebody's advisor, and it completely made sense that Betty was Marshall's. "You know," Marshall continued, seeing a nervous look cross Annie's face, "if you only wanted to see Betty, you didn't need to come all the way to Kalamazoo for that. She's in her office all the time."

"I know, but I wanted to see the session too," Annie mumbled in reply. Now that she was here, and staring down an entire weekend of sleeping in a sad dorm room and only talking to Marshall, her decision to come to the conference rather than just set up a meeting with Betty Randall back home felt increasingly ill-advised. She tried to push that thought out of her mind too and pretend she actually wanted to enjoy the conference.

"Have you met Betty?" Marshall asked.

"No. I was hoping to meet her tomorrow."

"You can meet her now if you want." They reached Valley Three, and Marshall was directing Annie to another door at the opposite end of the building from where registration took place. It was much less chaotic in this lobby, but Annie could hear the sound of voices chattering not too far away. "I'm actually supposed to meet her now — she's one of my dinner dates."

"Oh, well I don't want to interfere with your dinner," Annie said, making a show of looking around like there was a possibility she might know someone else and be able to excuse herself.

"This isn't dinner — this is wine hour. An opportunity for everyone to drink shitty boxed wine and mingle with other medievalists!"

He spread out his hands like he was offering her the world and Annie couldn't help but smile. Marshall was charming, in a totally non-sexual way. She wondered if that was why she had been so comfortable reading the grimoire with him that time.

She continued to follow Marshall down the hallway in the direction of the voices, which got louder and louder until they wound up in a crowded activity room that had cups of Franzia set up on folding tables all around the room.

"Here," Marshall said, holding out two cups of white wine to Annie.

Annie took one. "Thanks."

"No," Marshall said, pushing the second glass on her. "I'm handing you two. They go so fast that it's better to take two, in case they're all gone by the time you want a second glass."

Annie looked around. Many of the people in the room really were holding two wine glasses. She shook her head. "No thanks," she said. "That wine looks like it will give me a headache. I'll stick with one."

"Suit yourself," said Marshall, as he grabbed a second glass off a folding table and led the way out into the courtyard.

The sun had come out and it was actually kind of warm in the courtyard. Many of the medievalists had shed their jackets and shawls, and Annie wished she had left the blazer back in the dorm. Marshall stood on the threshold and scanned the crowd for his advisor. When he spotted her, he said, "Aha! There she is!" and grabbed Annie's hand around the wrist. Annie jerked her arm away and followed Marshall across the courtyard to a corner where the woman from the photograph on the university website appeared to be holding court among several other older-middle-aged women.

"And there's my student!" Betty announced in a loud voice when she caught sight of Marshall. "I'll catch up with you later, ladies."

The women dispersed and Marshall and Annie were able to take their places around Betty.

"Having a good conference so far, Betty?" Marshall asked.

"It's a whirlwind — as always. There are so many people for me to see and I'm always worried I'm not going to be able to catch up with all of them, or talk to all of them for as long as I would like. How is your conference so far, Marshall?" She still hadn't acknowledged Annie, who took a few steps back and started looking around the courtyard for pretend acquaintances.

"So far, so good," Marshall said to Betty. "I caught a couple good papers today, but I'm really looking forward to tomorrow, when all the poetry sessions are."

"And your paper!"

"And mine," Marshall conceded modestly. "This is Annie, by the way. She's a third-year history student at Michigan, working with Murray."

Annie turned around and stepped back into the circle. She was surprised Marshall remembered all that.

Betty looked Annie up and down. She was much taller than Annie, which automatically made this meeting seem like an evaluation. And she was squinting, the freckled skin around her eyes wrinkling inquisitively. Annie wasn't sure whether she was squinting because of the sun or because she was actually scrutinizing her, so she assumed it was the latter and tried not to look like a boring and immature student tagging along at a big people conference, which was exactly how she felt. She tugged at Gina's blazer, as if willing herself to look more important, but it didn't seem like it was going to help in this encounter — Betty was wearing a cotton dress in some frumpy pattern with tights and a big green scarf. She probably didn't even own a blazer.

"Ah. I think I've seen you at Medieval Lunches. Nice to formally meet you." She held out her hand, which Annie shook, immediately wishing her handshake was firmer. Then Betty turned back to Marshall.

"So who's all going to be at dinner?" Marshall asked.

"Stacy, Deb from Comp Lit, maybe one or two of their students, and then a recent grad — do you remember Steph Kang? — and another former student of Murray's." Betty nodded at Annie at the mention of her advisor. "Jamie Wilder. He's at Chicago now, and I'm not sure if he's bringing a student or not, and us. We reserved the entire back room at the British Empire, though, so there's room if you want to bring anyone."

That wasn't really an invitation, but charming, friendly Marshall took it as one. He turned to Annie and grinned. "So, do you want to come?" he asked. "Or do you have other dinner plans for tonight?" He knew the answer to that question. Annie hadn't left his side since they ran into each other a half hour ago.

"No, I don't want to intrude on your dinner," Annie replied.

"You're not intruding — I'm inviting you! Don't feel bad if you have other plans, though, but if you don't, then you're more than welcome to come with us." When Annie didn't say anything, Marshall turned to Betty and said, "You know, Annie has an interest in Arthurian Britain and she's been looking for an opportunity to talk to you about that new manuscript you found."

"Well I'm presenting on it tomorrow," Betty said. She was still squinting.

Annie wanted to run back to her room in Valley One and climb under that sad blanket to die. "I know. I plan to come to your session tomorrow," she managed to say. But now she wasn't so sure she would even make it to that.

"But dinner would be an excellent opportunity for you to get to know each other before then." Marshall's grin was back. "Come on, Annie — I insist." Annie thought about it for a split second. It wasn't dinner with just Marshall, it was dinner with a bunch of current and former Michigan people, and she was a Michigan person. And at any rate, it was probably better to accept the invitation than admit her alternative plans of dining alone.

"All right," she said finally.

Marshall's grin got bigger, if that was even possible. "Great! You can come with me in my car." Then he held up his empty wine glasses and gestured to the empty glasses in the hands of Annie and Betty. "Should we check and see if there's more wine?"

Betty held up a battered iPhone with cat stickers on it and squinted. "Wine's out," she said. "I just got a text. Shall we go to dinner?"

"Sure thing — see you at the restaurant!"

"It was nice to meet you," Annie tried to say to Betty as they turned to walk away, but Betty had already strode away.

| 5 |

The British Empire

Annie got into the passenger seat of Marshall's gray Pontiac Vibe and within minutes found herself in the heart of downtown Kalamazoo. Marshall parked at a meter on the left side of a four-lane one-way street and got out. "Where are we going?" Annie started to ask, but quickly followed up the question with a surprised, "Oh!" when she looked across the street at a storefront sporting a half-dozen British flags and just as many flags of former British colonies.

Marshall made another one of his grand arm movements as he started across the street. "The British Empire, milady."

Inside the restaurant, Annie could see she was in for a real themed experience. The "specials" menu, written on a chalkboard decked out in Union Jacks, featured fish pie and bangers and mash. The walls were hung with the flags of various British and colonial soccer teams. And on the front wall, right over the bar, hung the gigantic head of a rhinoceros wearing a pith helmet. Annie hoped it wasn't real.

"Back here," Marshall said, leading Annie to the back of the restaurant where he already spotted people he knew gathering in the private room. "Sorry we're not sitting by the rhino. We'll have to next year." He stopped for a moment and looked at Annie with his piercing blue eyes. "You will come to Kalamazoo next year, won't you?"

Annie glanced back up at the rhinoceros and smirked. "Maybe. I'll have to see how much I like it this year."

Once in the back room, Annie sat down toward the end of the table next to a chair with a purse on it and Marshall took his seat across from her. The pit in her stomach, which had vanished during the car ride, returned when the owner of the purse sat down and turned out to be Betty Randall. Annie turned to her right and saw a young Black man wearing a light green button-down shirt and his conference name badge pull out the chair beside her.

"Can I sit here?" he asked Annie.

She looked down at his name tag — Geoffrey Porter, he/him/his, University of Chicago — and back up at his warm, brown eyes that were still looking at Annie, waiting for her answer.

"Sure, uh, Geoffrey," Annie replied a second too late. She felt the pit in her stomach grow bigger. Great, she thought. A big deal professor who isn't sure if she has time to talk to me on my left and an attractive grad student who might even be dateable on my right. She was beginning to long for a table alone in the Valley cafeteria.

"You can call me Geoff," Geoff said, taking off his name badge and putting it in his pocket before sitting down.

"Annie."

"I'm a student of Jamie Wilder," Geoff continued. He gestured to the other side of the table at a balding man with animated eyebrows who was having a conversation with a younger man that Marshall also seemed to know. Annie vaguely wondered whether or not it would be worth networking with these people. Then she shuddered as she realized that that thought was the first time she ever used the word "network" as a verb.

"He graduated from Michigan about ten years ago and is taking me around to introduce me to early medieval people," Geoff continued. "He knows all of your profs here, but his own advisor isn't here. I guess he doesn't like to come to conferences."

"Murray Penge," Annie said, shaking thoughts of networking from her mind and turning back to Geoff. "Murray is my advisor."

"No way!" Geoff exclaimed. "What's he like? We'll have to talk more. I think Penge's work is fantastic. I was hoping I'd get to meet him here, but no such luck."

Great, Annie thought to herself again. A dateable guy who actually has something to talk about with me. She wasn't ready for this. She was grateful when the waitress came over to take drink orders. The waitress started on the other end of the table where the professors ordered everything from glasses of white wine to whiskey neat. When she got to Annie, Annie immediately said, "Gin and tonic."

"Interesting choice," Geoff commented after he had placed his order for a Michigan beer.

"We're at the British Empire," Annie said blankly. "There's a rhino with a pith helmet hanging on the wall over there. I literally don't think I could drink anything else."

Geoff opened his mouth to reply but just then Annie felt a hand on her left arm and turned to see Betty Randall suddenly taking an interest in her. She silently thanked Betty for saving her from an exchange she couldn't distinguish between a flirtation over drinks choices and friendly human interaction. Then her heart rate skyrocketed as the older woman put her on the spot.

"So Marshall tells me you're curious about the manuscript I found and whether it might shed some light on this old grimoire of yours purporting to contain the Lost Sigils of King Arthur," she said.

Annie frowned. She hadn't mentioned anything about the book or the sigils to Marshall at all that day, and Marshall hadn't said anything about them to her, either. He presumed correctly, but Annie felt like he was presuming too much and sharing information that wasn't his to share. Eager to make up for her awkwardness with Betty earlier, though, Annie perked up and said, "Yes — I have no idea what these sigils or the text around them mean, but they don't seem to belong to the grimoire at all. They look like they're on much older parchment and were just bound into the center of the grimoire."

Betty pursed her lips together, thinking. "Hmm," she said after a moment. "Do you have the grimoire with you?"

"No, but —"

Before Annie could mention all the photos she'd taken with her phone, Betty said, "Well that's not very helpful to us then, is it?"

"I — I took —" Annie blustered. "I'm looking forward to your talk tomorrow," she mumbled. "Maybe you'll mention something that looks like some of the text on the parchment pieces and we can talk about it afterwards."

"Do you at least have photos?" Betty pressed.

"*Yes*," said Annie. Moving quickly, she reached into the pocket of Gina's blazer and pulled out her phone before Betty could say anything else.

Betty put on her glasses — blue cat-eye — and took Annie's phone out of her hand. Now Marshall and Geoff were watching them. Annie sat back in her chair and waited for Betty to be done with her phone.

"You know, I have to admit I hadn't heard about the Lost Sigils of King Arthur until Marshall here told me about them awhile back," Betty muttered to herself without looking up from the phone. Marshall was beaming. "I joked with him that it was some bullshit conspiracy theory stuff," Betty continued. "But all the same, if we had the pages here... Well not *here* here, but in a lab, we could have them carbon dated and determine whether these pages are actually ancient or if they're a hoax from the time the grimoire was produced, or even a modern hoax." She looked over at Annie. "Do you have any photos of the binding?"

"No," Annie started, but Marshall interrupted, "Do you really think you can get a grant to carbon date those pages?" His voice sounded higher and more eager, like it did when he first looked at the grimoire with Annie. He leaned over the table, nearly missing smearing his sweater in the little pats of butter that sat on a plate in front of him.

Betty glared at Marshall over her glasses. "I just discovered an entirely new seventh-century manuscript that mentions King Arthur. I can get a grant for fucking anything."

"That is true," Marshall agreed smugly, sitting back in his chair.

The drinks arrived, and Annie started to feel more at ease talking to Betty about the pages in the grimoire. She walked her through the photos on her phone, and she and Marshall together showed her their transcription and translation of the text around the sigils. Geoff eventually got bored of talking to the English grad student who sat across from him and joined in the conversation as well, mostly asking questions about paleography and Latin translation.

Toward the end of the meal, Betty pushed aside her shepherd's pie and picked up Annie's phone again. She was squinting at the photo of her translation. "What do you think all this means," she said, "about the memory?" *Let us scorn the memory of Arthur.*

"I don't know," Annie admitted. "I kind of agree with you about the conspiracy theory stuff, and it would be helpful if we could date these pages. I actually found them and read them over two years ago and then totally forgot about them until I saw that you found that new manuscript."

Betty took another bite of her dinner and chewed thoughtfully. "I'm sorry, Annie," she said finally, "but I don't think I can help you." There was a crease in between her eyes that only got deeper as she continued to stare at the photo. "The manuscript I found is a poem about Arthur and the valiant deeds of him and his men against Mordred at Camlann. It's significant because it's now the oldest reference to Camlann, and it also states explicitly that Mordred fought *against* Arthur at that battle. But it doesn't mention anything about sigils or memory or Arthur murdering entire peoples. Arthur's the good guy in my text."

Annie's face fell. She didn't think she'd be that disappointed to hear that Betty's manuscript was unrelated, but now that she was hearing it she felt really let down. "Well, I still want to hear more about it tomorrow," she said politely. "Maybe the other papers in the session, or questions by some of the Arthurian scholars attending your paper, could shed some light on my text."

Annie felt weird saying "my text" the way Betty did. Betty had a right to call the manuscript "hers" — she had found it, hadn't she? Annie had been given hers by her advisor. She wondered whether Murray even knew those weird pages were lodged inside the grimoire he had given her at their first meeting. He probably did, she concluded, but he didn't care. Murray was like that.

Betty didn't seem to take issue with the possessive language Annie used to describe her text, though. She just said, "It could be. But I wouldn't hold out too much hope for the other papers in my session. I've seen one of them present before, and her research is really not very strong, to put it lightly. And the other is good, but he's not actually an Arthur person and his paper is on pedagogy. It should be interesting, but probably not what you're looking for."

"I know someone who might know something about your manuscript pages, Annie, or at least be able to rough date them without having to do any expensive tests." Annie looked up in the direction of the voice on the other side of Marshall. The speaker was Jamie Wilder, Geoff's advisor. Murray's student. Which made him her...academic big brother? Academia was weird.

"Who?" Annie and Betty asked at the same time.

"Mary Kay McKinley!"

"Oh shit, Mary Kay," Betty whispered, reaching in her purse for her phone. "There's another one I was supposed to get in contact with and probably won't have time to see. But she's in your field, Jamie. She doesn't even do England."

"She doesn't, but she hit upon something weird in Jordanes last year and has been chasing it ever since. She presented on it at Shifting Frontiers in Late Antiquity a couple months ago. I think she's giving a version of that paper here, with more stuff added. As of March, she had found references to the same weird signs in Jordanes, Venantius Fortunatus, and some Byzantine author, and they're all related to some mass-murderer running around in England."

Annie and Betty looked at each other. Then Betty turned on her phone screen and started texting vigorously.

"What kind of weird signs?" Marshall asked Jamie, his voice high again. "Could they have been sigils?"

Jamie shrugged. "No idea. Honestly, I don't remember much of Shifting Frontiers. All the sessions are plenary, so after sitting through forty different papers in three days, I'm lucky that I even remembered that much about Mary Kay's paper. If you're interested, you should see her present this weekend. I think she's on Saturday, in one of the *Early Medieval Europe* sessions."

"She's going to be at Valley Three at nine o'clock," Betty said definitively as she put away her phone. She turned to Annie and said,

"If you want to go there after dinner, I can introduce you. I need to meet up with her anyway."

"Sure!" replied Annie. "I'm staying in Valley One so I need to go that way anyway."

"Don't tell me you didn't know about the night receptions," Marshall said, gleeful to have something to contribute to the conversation.

Betty snorted. "'Reception' is a generous term for what goes on in Valley Three."

Marshall ignored her and continued, "Big university presses host receptions in Valley Three on Thursday and Friday nights. Everybody goes."

"Not everybody," Betty said disdainfully. "Once you reach a certain age you realize there are better places to spend your evenings at Kalamazoo. I had thought Mary Kay would have reached that age already — she has to be forty by now, hasn't she?"

"Some people never reach that age," Jamie chimed in. "I saw Edward Thomas at one last year, and he's an even bigger deal than you are, Betty."

Betty scowled at that last comment, and Annie couldn't help but look over at Marshall and smile. He was grinning back.

"I'd like to come along and meet Mary Kay McKinley, too," Geoff said on Annie's right. "I'm writing a chapter on Venantius Fortunatus and it would be great to talk to her about it."

"That's great!" Annie said before burying her face in the dessert menu.

| 6 |

Valley Three at Night

An hour later, Annie was back in the passenger seat of the Pontiac with Betty riding along in the cramped back seat. Betty wasn't wearing her seatbelt and kept making Annie nervous by sticking her head into the front seat to make some comment. About Deb from Comp Lit judging her for going back to the Valleys after dinner; about how she couldn't believe Mary Kay McKinley came back to Kalamazoo this year, since she only did late antique conferences lately; about how *dare* Mary Kay not tell her about the references she found to a mass-murderer in early medieval England. Annie was glad when they finally got back to campus just so she could have a break from listening to Betty.

"Stop!" Betty yelled when Marshall pulled into the Valley Three parking lot. Marshall slammed on the break and Betty had to brace herself on Annie's chair to keep from flying through the windshield. "There she is — up on the porch to the first entrance!"

"Hold your horses," Marshall said as he eased up on the break and started looking for a parking spot. "I'm sure she's not going anywhere."

Marshall found a spot in the back of the lot by the second entrance to the dorm and the three of them walked back down to the first entrance to join the group of people Betty had spotted when they first arrived. They were still several yards away from the porch when Betty touched Annie's shoulder and said, "There she is. You can't miss her."

At first Annie had no idea what Betty was talking about. There were at least eight people sitting and standing around a picnic table in front of the dorm entrance. Then she realized that all of them were men in suit jackets except for one woman wearing a blue and green flowered dress and silver pumps. She had streaky blond hair pulled back in a French twist and was holding a cigarette in one hand and some kind of mixed drink in the other. Betty was right — you couldn't miss her.

"Aaaaand she's drunk already," Betty continued. "For fuck's sake, it's barely nine, how can she be drunk already?'

"How can you tell?" asked Annie.

"The cigarette is a dead giveaway. She's the basicest basic-bitch I've ever met. 'I only smoke when I'm drunk!'" she mocked. But the second Betty reached the end of the stairs, she changed her tone completely and shouted up at the picnic table, "Mary Kay McKinley, it's been too long! Two years, now? Three?"

"Do mine eyes deceive me?" Mary Kay shouted back, turning in her seat to face Betty. Her eyes were wide and her bright pink lips were stretched into a radiant smile. "Or is it truly Betty Randall in the flesh, deigning to grace us lowly drinkers of the Valley Three Free Booze with her immaculate presence?"

"Ha ha," Betty said sarcastically while smiling right back. When she got to the top of the stairs, she reached out and pulled Mary Kay into a tight hug, giving no heed to the drink and cigarette the younger woman still held in her hand, and Mary Kay hugged her back.

"But seriously, Betty," said Mary Kay, brushing herself off. "I haven't seen you near a Valley after dinner since, well, ever."

"Important business brings me here tonight," replied Betty, gesturing to Annie and Marshall down on the sidewalk. "These two grad students came across an interesting text that mentions King Arthur. *And* we just heard that *you* have been chasing a King Arthur trail of your own through Venantius Fortunatus and Jordanes and whoever else late antique that you read. Why didn't you tell me?"

Mary Kay nodded conspiratorially and glanced over Betty's shoulder at Annie and Marshall, who were still standing at the bottom of the stairs. "Is that them?" she asked, waving.

"Yeah." Betty turned around and waved again. "Get up here, you guys!"

Annie and Marshall came up the stairs and stood awkwardly next to the picnic table where two men in full suits had started playing quarter bounce. Mary Kay moved closer to Betty and grabbed onto her arm. "You know, Betty, I could say the same to you, about not telling me. I had to find out about your manuscript discovery from god damn Twitter!" She started laughing and tripped backward into one of the men at the table who caught her with ease.

"Hey, watch it with that thing, MK, you're going to set my hair on fire!" he said.

"Sorry." Mary Kay took one last drag on her cigarette before stubbing it out on the side of the metal table and dropping it into what looked like a plastic baggy lined with aluminum foil.

"Isn't WMU a tobacco-free campus now?" Betty asked.

"Yeah? That's why we're packing out." Betty pointed to the makeshift ash tray and raised an eyebrow. Mary Kay shrugged. "What? I have three boys under the age of twelve — I'm used to packing out weird shit in my bag."

Betty finally turned back to the grad students and said, "Marshall? Annie? I would like to introduce you to a former student of mine. She was one of my undergrads when I worked at Loyola Maryland. Mary Kay McKinley."

"It's a pleasure to meet you," said Mary Kay. She stepped away from the picnic table, a little unsteady on her high heels. "Let's get away from these clowns. They're all drunk."

"Not my fault!" called out the larger of the two men at the picnic table. "It was the Carolingianists' idea to buy shots at the early medieval dinner!"

"You know we Carolingianists always have more fun!" shouted back a tall man with orange hair who was standing behind the table smoking over his own piece of tin foil.

Mary Kay ignored them and turned to look at Annie. "Sorry," she said quickly. "Now tell me about this text you found. Where'd you find it?"

Annie took a deep breath. This must be what people did at Kalamazoo — talk about serious medieval topics while other medievalists played drinking games in the background. "It's bound in an early-modern grimoire..." she started to say.

"It contains the Lost Sigils of King Arthur!" Marshall exclaimed at the same time.

Annie glared at Marshall and made herself keep talking while Mary Kay glanced back and forth from one to the other. "It's two old pages of parchment that don't seem to match the rest of the book. They have some strange writing on them — sigils, I guess — and a hand-written Latin inscription all around the sigils. I can show you." She started to reach into her pocket for her phone.

"You don't have the codex pages in there!" Mary Kay shrieked.

"Calm down, Mary Kay," said Betty. "Some of us keep our phones close to us in our pockets rather than in our giant-ass mom bags."

"Hey!" said Mary Kay. "Don't knock the mom bag until you try it. With this bag, I am prepared for every eventuality. Packing out cigarette butts? No problem. I even have Febreze in here for when I need to rejoin civilization. Which is looking to be pretty soon." She held up her empty drink glass and set it down on the picnic table.

"What, you don't have a flask in there?" Betty teased.

"Oh, of course I do. But I'm not going to use it up now when there's perfectly good free booze inside. I'm saving it for the dance."

"Hey, Mary Kay, speaking of drinks," said one of the Carolingianists on the other side of the table. "We're just about to head out to Waldo's as soon as Danny finishes his beer. You late antiquers want to join us?"

"Why do you guys want to drive your car to a place where you have to pay money for drinks when there are free ones right here in our dormitory?"

Danny the orange-haired Carolingianist shrugged. "It's tradition."

"*Your* tradition," one of the late antiquers at the table corrected in a British accent.

"Yeah," added Mary Kay. "I'm staying here to talk to these grad students."

"Suit yourself." Most of the people on the porch waved goodbye and took off down the stairs, leaving only the two guys seated at the picnic table. Mary Kay, Betty, Annie, and Marshall went back to join them.

"Annie and Marshall?" said Mary Kay. "This is Andrew Levine and Dave DeCecco. They're late antique historians, like me. Betty, I believe you already know them?"

Dave DeCecco nodded to Betty and said, "It's great to see you again. Come sit down."

Betty took a seat beside Dave and Mary Kay stood between Annie and Marshall. "Now," she said, "let's have a look at those photos."

Annie fumbled in her pocket for her phone and held it out. Mary Kay hovered over her shoulder. She was shorter than Annie, but her heels made them about the same height. Annie was glad when she found the photos and Mary Kay took the phone from her hand, no longer hovering.

Mary Kay held the phone out in the middle of the table so her colleagues could see the photos. Betty leaned over to look, too, even though she had already seen them. For a long time, Mary Kay squinted at the screen and stared a little blearily. Finally, she asked, "Those are your symbols, in the middle?"

"Yeah," said Annie and Marshall together.

"And there's the inscription." She tapped a blue painted fingernail on the Latin text around the sigils and stared a little more. Dave and Andrew nodded but didn't say anything. "I suppose this description *could* match the killer Fortunatus described, but I'll have to look at it again tomorrow when I have more time to concentrate." Yeah, and when you're not totally wasted, thought Annie. Mary Kay was not as impressive as she'd been led to believe. "Do you want to meet for breakfast before the keynote?"

"Sure," Annie said.

"Betty?"

"Yeah, all right," Betty replied. "But I actually want to see tomorrow's keynote, so we'll have to meet early. Is seven okay?"

"Seven a.m. in the Valley Dining Center," Mary Kay repeated. "Got that, everyone?" Annie and Marshall both nodded. Betty smirked.

Mary Kay turned back to the phone and held it up to her face, her lips pursed tightly together. "I'm really not sure about these —

what did you call them? Symbols? I've never heard of the Lost Symbols of King Arthur, except maybe in a Dan Brown novel I read one time. But I'm not really an Arthur person, or even an image person, for that matter." She handed the phone back to Annie. "You know who would really like to see these images?" she asked. "Gavin."

Annie had no idea who Gavin was, but Andrew looked up and said, "Gavin Chen? I haven't seen him yet. I thought he would be at the early medieval dinner, but he wasn't. I don't even think he's in the program this year."

"That's odd," Mary Kay said. "He's always here."

Dave shrugged and said, "I haven't seen him either. Maybe he took the year off."

Then Mary Kay turned to Betty and asked, almost accusingly, "Where is Gavin?"

Betty looked down, momentarily lacking confidence for the first time since Annie met her. "I don't know. Why should I know?" she asked defensively.

"I don't know, but Gavin *would* like to see these images. He might actually be able to identify them." She looked at her watch. "It's a little late now, but I'll call him tomorrow. He should be here, or at least take a look at Annie's photos." She pulled a pen and paper out of her tote bag and wrote in a sloppy cursive, "Breakfast, 7 am, Valley," and under it, "Call Gavin and tell him to get his ass up here."

"Gavin Chen?" called a voice from the parking lot. Annie turned when she heard the familiar voice. It was Jamie Wilder, from dinner, and Geoff was walking beside him. Geoff looked up at Annie and waved. Annie didn't wave back.

"Jamie!" Dave called, standing up to greet his friend. "You made it! We missed you at the early medieval dinner!"

Jamie bounded up the stairs and did the awkward handshake hug thing to Andrew and Dave and wedged himself in between them at the table. These men were forty-year-old versions of all the guys she knew in college, Annie thought with distaste. She wondered why Mary Kay hung out with them.

"Sorry guys," Jamie was saying. "I wanted to catch up with my old Michigan people. This is my student, Geoff Porter. Geoff? These are the late antique historians I was telling you about. You should get to know them — these three are awesome."

"You flatter us, Jamie," Mary Kay said, grinning.

Geoff stepped up onto the porch beside Annie and whispered, "Have you gotten to talk to Mary Kay McKinley yet?"

"Just now," whispered Annie.

"Is she amazing or what?" Geoff asked. " Her scholarship on early medieval popular culture is so interesting. I pretty much want to be her when I grow up."

Annie gave Geoff a curious look, and he grinned.

"The Black, male, millennial version of her, obviously."

Annie laughed nervously and turned toward Betty, who was looking at the activity tracker on her wrist. She had been looking down at it ever since Gavin's name came up, and Annie was pretty sure she wasn't checking to see if she hit her steps goal.

"All right," said Betty, "it's nine-thirty and I told Angela Dee I'd meet her at the Radisson for drinks now. But I'll see you all at breakfast tomorrow morning." Her eyes lingered on Annie's for a moment and Annie breathed a sigh of relief. Even if Mary Kay didn't make it in the morning, at least Betty would be there.

"Great! See you in the morning!" said Mary Kay. "I can't believe I get to catch up with you *twice* in one Kalamazoo." Betty smiled and hugged Mary Kay again. Annie thought she saw Betty whisper something in Mary Kay's ear, but she couldn't hear what it was. Then Betty bade her and Marshall goodbye and took off down the stairs.

"Now I need to get inside for another drink before there's only shitty beer left," said Mary Kay once Betty was gone.

"You don't strike me as the kind of person who would be a snob about free beer," Jamie observed.

"Oh, I'm not," Mary Kay replied. "But that's beside the point. Why settle for shitty beer when you could be having crap gin?" She carefully sealed up the ash tray bag and dropped it in her tote and straightened out her skirt. "You coming, guys?"

"Sure" said Geoff. "I would love to talk to you about Venantius Fortunatus. I'm writing a chapter on him and depictions of violence in especially his biographical poems and am really interested to hear your thoughts about that."

"Of course! Geoff, is it? I could talk about Fortunatus for hours!"

Geoff looked back at Annie. "You coming?" he asked.

Annie looked over at Marshall. She must have been visibly uncomfortable, because Marshall took a step toward her and said quietly, just to her, "It's still early — we should go inside and get a drink. We can go to the other side of Valley Three if you want, though. We don't have to hang out with these late antique historians anymore. I don't really belong here anyway."

Annie thought for a moment about Marshall's proposal and couldn't think of anything she would rather do less. She also didn't want to hurt Geoff's feelings by staying out but not with him. He seemed nice and she didn't want to be rude to him on purpose. She looked over at Geoff who was waiting expectantly, turned back to Marshall and said, "No thank you. I'm pretty tired. I'm going to go to bed early so I'm ready for that seven a.m. breakfast tomorrow. I'll see you then."

"Have a good night's sleep, Annie," Geoff said. "Maybe I'll catch you at breakfast too."

Annie tried to smile as she said goodbye once again to Geoff and Marshall and the late antique history professors, but she had a sneaking suspicion that she had used up all her good smiles for the day and it looked more like a grimace. Then she started up the hill toward Valley One, relieved to have made it through her first day at Kalamazoo relatively unscathed.

| 7 |

Dawn at Kalamazoo

Annie wasn't sure if she had actually fallen asleep when the alarm on her phone rang at six fifteen. Her night in the Valley One dorm bed was one of the worst night's sleeps she had ever had, and that was counting the first few nights in her own freshman dorm. She determined she must have been asleep for a little bit, though, because she was shivering under her thin blanket and didn't remember being so cold a moment ago. She got up, stretched (she didn't remember being so stiff a moment ago, either), and made her way to the bathroom, hoping against hope that whoever was staying in the room on the other side wouldn't be in there. They weren't, so Annie hurried inside and showered as quickly as she could in the tiny stall. At least the water was hot. She put on one of Gina's dresses, plain green, and the blazer, and hurried down to breakfast.

Marshall was waiting for her in the Valley One lobby. They hadn't planned to meet up before breakfast, but Annie wasn't surprised to see him. She was also a little relieved at having someone to walk into the dining hall with. The dining hall appeared humongous from the outside.

"Do you have your phone?" Marshall asked.

"Huh?" Annie felt the pocket of her blazer to make sure it was there, even though she knew it was.

"For the photos. Betty and Mary Kay might want to see them again."

"Oh, yeah." Good morning to you, too, Marshall.

"Where are we supposed to meet them?" Annie asked when they were halfway down the hill to the Valley Dining Hall.

"I don't know. I have Betty's phone number if we can't find them."

Marshall didn't have to call Betty, though. Once again, Mary Kay McKinley was impossible to miss. She was standing right by the entrance to the dining hall wearing the same blond French twist and silver pumps as last night, this time with a dark gray blazer and black pants and Ray Bans. Betty was standing next to her in another patterned dress and scarf, chatting away cheerfully.

"There they are!" Betty shouted as soon as she spotted Annie and Marshall. Mary Kay recoiled.

Inside the dining hall was even huger than the outside. Annie walked behind Betty, who blazed a trail through a veritable maze of tables and food stations that seemed to stretch on forever. Finally, Betty found a table for four and set her purse on it. Without a word, she turned back in the other direction, presumably to find some food. Annie set down her conference bag and did the same.

She returned to the table a few moments later with a cup of coffee and a sparse plate of eggs, sausage, and an English muffin to find Mary Kay sitting alone, picking at a scone and trying and failing to take a sip of her orange juice. Up close and without her sunglasses, Mary Kay looked terrible. Her eyes were puffy and her skin had a grayish tinge. Annie felt an instant pang of compassion for how pathetic she was at that moment.

"Do you want me to get you a banana?" Annie asked. "That might taste okay and make you feel a little better."

Mary Kay smiled appreciatively. "No thank you. I'll be all right," she said in a hoarse voice. "I just couldn't fall asleep last night. I think once I get a chance to nap my body will be able to heal itself a little."

"Those dorm beds really are horrible," Annie agreed.

"I know. Every year I tell myself I'm going to stay in the hotel, and every year I just want to party in Valley Three and then walk up to my room." She shrugged and took the tiniest of bites of her scone. "One day I'll grow up."

Annie smiled. For some reason, she was comforted by the fact that even big deal professors with three boys under twelve still didn't feel like grownups sometimes. That took a little pressure off her. And it made the professors a little bit easier to talk to.

Just then, Marshall and Betty arrived at the table with their plates full of cafeteria breakfast and started chowing down. Betty's plate was heaped with everything the dining hall had to offer, all slathered in a suspicious-looking sausage gravy. Mary Kay looked like she was going to be sick.

"Rough night?" Betty asked with a smile. "I slept great, and I'm ready to take on the day!"

Mary Kay scowled. "I would be fine if I had been able to fall asleep."

"Maybe you would have if you had slept in an actual bed," Betty suggested. "Or if you hadn't taken those shots at dinner."

"It wasn't the shots. Seriously, I would be fine, I even turned in before one, but I was just wired from all the energy of seeing so many friends at once, so many conversations going through my head. I met a really smart grad student who made me think harder about Venantius Fortunatus than I had in awhile. So I couldn't sleep. Tossed and turned all night, and then my alarm went off." She shrugged, tried to take another bite of the scone, thought better of it and set it back down.

Annie was sure Mary Kay was telling the truth. She looked defeated under her crisp outfit and fresh makeup, like she had done all she could to be ready for another day at the conference but couldn't quite manage it.

"Anyway, I've felt worse at Kalamazoo. This is nothing like the time Janice Stark gave the keynote and it took every ounce of strength I had not to vomit in my tote bag during her very good talk."

Betty made a face. "I don't know why you hang out with those late antique guys," she said, her voice scornful.

"I'm a Roman historian, posing as a medievalist. Whom else is there to hang out with?"

"Good point," said Betty, turning back to her plate.

The group ate in silence for a moment until Annie finished her breakfast. It was now seven-thirty, and the keynote started at eight-thirty but it was all the way up the stairs in Bernhard. She didn't want to waste any more time. She needed to talk to these professors about the codex pages, and she had to do it now before she lost all the confidence she gained seeing Mary Kay so vulnerable, and Betty so hungry.

Fumbling around in her tote for her phone, Annie cleared her throat and said, "So, I know you both looked at these photos last night, but I wondered whether you wanted to look at them again now. You know, um, together, and —" She looked pityingly over at Mary Kay who wasn't making eye contact. "In the light of day."

"Sure," Mary Kay said, holding out her hand. She glanced over at Betty and her half-full plate, smirking, and said, "I'll go first so she can finish breakfast."

Betty glared back at Mary Kay but didn't say anything.

Annie looked at Marshall, but he didn't seem to notice. He was trying to look over at the phone in front of Mary Kay without dripping syrup all over his suit.

Mary Kay scrolled through the photos in silence, concentrating on each one before moving on to the next. When she got to the photo of the transcription and translation that Annie and Marshall had done, she paused and looked up.

"What is it?" asked Marshall. "Did I transcribe it wrong?"

Mary Kay shook her head, her eyebrows furrowed. "No, you transcribed it perfectly. But this line here, 'Cruel Arthur killed a thousand nations' — that's in Jordanes, almost verbatim. It doesn't say 'Arthur,' but everything else is the same, down to word-order." Her brown eyes were suddenly bright. "And '*homicida*' to describe a British lord — that's in Fortunatus. And both those references also mention 'signs.' I thought the signs they were referring to were portents, but they could be literal signs or symbols too."

Annie gasped and looked at Marshall, who was grinning from ear to ear.

"There's other stuff about a British warlord who murdered entire peoples in the sixth century in Photius" Mary Kay continued. "I'll have to look at the Photius text again, but I think the details are the same. And this mention of Mordred —"

"Mordred?" Betty almost spit out her food. "*My* text mentions Mordred." Betty snatched Annie's phone from Mary Kay's hand and started looking at the translation. "How did we not talk about the last part of the translation yesterday?" She put on her glasses and started to read, "'Cruel Arthur killed a thousand nations, yeah yeah... even Mordred could not save them.' Fuck," she whispered. "*Fuck.* We have to get these pages dated. I need to know if they're older than my manuscript."

Mary Kay took the phone back from Betty and swiped back to the photos of the manuscript. Marshall followed the phone with his eyes like he was watching the most unbelievable tennis match he had ever seen.

"Hmm, I'm not an expert in Latin paleography," Mary Kay said, "but this looks pre-miniscule. It's either seventh, eighth century, or a forgery." She looked at Annie and asked, "Is this parchment? Did you bring it with you?"

Annie shook her head, wishing more than ever that she hadn't left the book behind with Gina. She hadn't realized how important the object itself would be to these scholars. She had thought it would be more important to protect it. But without the actual pages in front of them, neither Betty nor Mary Kay could say anything more than, "It might be real, or it might be a forgery."

Betty was still frowning. "The manuscript I found explicitly presents Mordred as an opponent to Arthur at the Battle of Camlann. If this text is real — if Arthur really was a killer of nations and Mordred was trying to defend entire peoples from him — that changes things for my text." She looked over at Annie and continued, "I was telling you yesterday — Arthur's made out to be a good guy. But the details of the narrative are surprisingly gory and in some places a little twisted. It's completely different from other early poems about Arthur, and this context helps explain why."

"And if the references that I've been finding are echoing Annie's inscriptions," Mary Kay said, "then they must be talking about the event that Betty's text describes. People knew about it all over the world, and maybe these signs have something to do with it." She gestured with Annie's phone. "I have to check Photius."

"Now?" Betty asked, looking at her watch.

Mary Kay brought her hand up to her head. "No, not now. But definitely before my paper tomorrow. I think I want to change some things."

Betty nodded and turned back to the last of her breakfast. Annie was a little disappointed that no one mentioned Gavin Chen — she really thought an archaeologist who might have seen the sigils before would be really helpful to all three (four) of them, but there was no way she was going to say that man's name in front of Betty unprovoked. Not after she made so much progress talking to Betty. They were almost like colleagues, now, discussing the codex. Annie sighed. They still had two more days at the conference, and Mary Kay was about to go do more research before her paper the next day. Maybe she would find something more concrete about the signs and remember she was supposed to call Gavin.

At last, Betty finished her breakfast and stood up. "Okay, we have to get to the keynote. You guys coming?"

"Right behind you!" said Marshall, finishing his last few bites of sausage. "Come on, Annie."

Without saying a word — she was still processing the conversation they had just finished — Annie picked up her plate and started to follow Betty and Marshall out of the dining hall.

"I think I'm going to skip the keynote," said Mary Kay, who was still seated.

"No shit," said Betty. "The keynote speaker's a good one, but he's no Janice Stark. Get some sleep."

"I'll see you at your session later," was all Mary Kay said in return.

Annie gave Mary Kay an extra smile. Why was Betty so mean to her? she wondered. She thought they were good friends, after the way they kept hugging last night, but maybe that was just a performance. Annie turned around to see Betty several strides ahead of Marshall at the tray return station. Was Betty only pretending she liked Mary Kay? Or was she pretending she didn't like her? Betty was a strange woman.

It was cold outside and Annie had to pull Gina's blazer tightly around herself to keep warm. She was wearing footless leggings with a pair of ballet flats and really wished she had on her Doc Martens and a pair of nice, thick socks instead. She looked longingly up at Valley One when they passed it, but Betty was now a hundred yards ahead of her. "Are you coming to the keynote?" asked Marshall, who had started jogging to catch up to his advisor.

"Yeah," said Annie. "Well actually, I wanted to ask Betty something, but I don't think I'm going to be able to catch up to her."

"No, probably not. Betty's so busy, and she knows so many people. She probably has to meet someone before the keynote and didn't tell us when she planned breakfast with us. She does that a lot." Marshall sighed. "It's kind of annoying, really. She always says she's going to take me places and introduce me to people at conferences, and she *does*, sort of. I mean, she took us to dinner last night. But then she always has more important people to talk to and forgets about me."

Annie shrugged. "At least your advisor *comes* to conferences. I don't think Murray's been to Kalamazoo in anyone's recent memory."

Marshall turned up the hill towards Betty. Annie pulled the blazer more tightly around herself as she glanced back toward Valley One and the prospect of more comfortable clothing.

"Hey Annie!" someone shouted from the direction of Valley Two.

Oh no, thought Annie, when she realized she was staring right at Geoff, who was jogging to catch up with her. He was wearing a blue sweater over a white collared shirt and he looked so professional and comfortable. Annie was immediately glad she was wearing the green dress and ballet flats for her run-in with Geoff, and just as immediately frustrated with herself for actually wanting to appear traditionally attractive to a guy she didn't even want to date.

"Are you going to the keynote?" Geoff asked when he reached her.

"Yeah!" Marshall answered. "You coming too?"

Geoff nodded and smiled. Annie didn't realize the keynote address — by some later medieval literature person she had never heard of — was so smile-worthy. But she found herself smiling back at Geoff for no reason. His smile was just so inviting. Much kinder than Chadwick's smile, which was all pointy and manipulative and didn't include his eyes.

Annie shook her head to clear the Chad away. She had been doing such a good job of not thinking about her college boyfriend recently, and was annoyed to find him cropping up now, while she was at a conference smiling at a guy who seemed to be, in every way, the complete opposite of Chad. "I'm not going to the keynote," she answered.

"You're not?" asked Marshall.

Annie shook her head again. She wanted to make sure Geoff knew that shaking was a "no" and not an insane attempt to shake some stray bad thoughts out of her head. "No, I didn't get enough sleep last night and want to rest up for the sessions later." At least that wasn't a total lie.

Geoff nodded, still smiling. "I understand. I'm not really into the keynote either, but I told Jamie I'd meet him there so I'm kind of obligated. I'll probably see you later, though. Are you going to the 'Arthuriana' session?"

That was Betty's session. "Yeah," said Annie reluctantly. "I guess I'll see you there." She waved goodbye — more to Marshall than to Geoff — and turned up the path to Valley One, wondering what she was going to do with herself for the next six hours before Betty's session.

| 8 |

Arthuriana

After braving the Valley Dining Hall by herself for lunch — a feat that was much worse in the anticipation than in the actual deed — Annie got out her campus map for the first time since the evening before and navigated to Bernhard. Bernhard was a large building right in the middle of campus, positioned rather incongruously across a quad from a beautiful old Italianate house that didn't seem to match the rest of the campus. Annie arrived early for Betty's session, so she momentarily debated exploring the house, but panicked and went inside Bernhard instead. She still had to figure out what room the session was meeting in.

She arrived in the room about fifteen minutes early. The 1:30 session was the first session after lunch, though, so the room was empty except for three people who each occupied a different corner of the classroom. Annie was about to take the fourth when one of the people looked up and waved her over. It was Geoff.

Annie surprised herself by smiling at Geoff as she entered the room. She sat down beside him and didn't let it bother her when he wanted to spend the next fifteen minutes talking. He was a familiar face, anyway. A good face, Annie found herself thinking. She could totally date him, she decided. But only if she asked him first, when she was ready. And she was nowhere near ready.

Geoff had his laptop open to a blank Word document. At the top of the page was one word: "Arthuriana." The name of the session. Annie got out her laptop. She guessed this was what people did at conferences. She had only brought along the laptop so she could show people photos of the codex without having to pass around her phone. She guessed she should probably take notes, too. Especially on Betty's paper, if it explained the context of her text.

"I wasn't going to come to this session, but Mary Kay McKinley convinced me that I should come hear about Betty Randall's manuscript find," Geoff said to Annie, a little quietly so as not to attract the attention of other King Arthur enthusiasts who were now starting to fill the room. "It's not really what I do, though. I'm more of a Merovingian Francia guy. Actually a little bit later than Arthur. Late-sixth, seventh centuries."

"This is the only session I came for," Annie replied. Then realizing it would be polite to give Geoff some explanation, she added, "but it's not really what I do, either. My dissertation's going to be about women's monasteries in Gaul and Italy, maybe North Africa. I sort of fell into this King Arthur stuff when my advisor — Murray — gave me that grimoire with those weird pages in it that I've been showing everybody."

"That's so amazing," said Geoff, genuinely impressed. "You're actually making a new discovery. How does it feel?"

Annie shrugged. She didn't feel amazing. She was in awe of Geoff's courage at being able to walk right up to a scholar he admired and start asking her questions about his research. She couldn't believe that *he* would think *she* was doing something amazing. "I don't know," she answered. "Like I'm not the one making the discovery. Betty made a discovery. Mary Kay made a discovery. I just found this weird text that somehow connects the two, and we're not even sure it's not a forgery."

"Well if it is a forgery, that means *somebody* saw a connection between all those other references, or at least saw something weird and *made* a connection."

Annie thought a moment. Geoff had a point. "I guess you're right. I should pursue this text. But it still feels a little weird."

"In what way?"

"Well, I own the text, because Murray gave me the book, but it was actually Marshall who was interested and wanted to read it. And I couldn't even have read the letters if Marshall hadn't transcribed them for me first."

Now it was Geoff's turn to shrug. His shrug was much more relaxed than Annie's, like it was an acknowledgment of freedom rather than defeat. "So you and Marshall made a discovery together. But that doesn't make it any less yours."

As if summoned by mention of his name, Marshall entered the room next, closely followed by Mary Kay, who looked much more alive than she did that morning.

"Hey guys!" Marshall said to Annie and Geoff. "Thanks for saving me a seat." He took the seat on Annie's other side, and Mary Kay filed in beside Marshall, reaching out her hand to wave at Annie. Annie waved back, not sure if she should say anything.

Annie looked to the front of the room and saw that Betty had arrived and was standing near the podium talking to the other presenters. She looked at her watch — it was almost time for the session to begin.

"Welcome to the second session of the day, 'Arthuriana,'" said a mousy-looking woman in quiet voice. The microphone on the podium didn't work. That wouldn't be an issue for Betty, though, Annie thought. "Today, we have three papers on a variety of different subjects in the field of Arthurian Studies. First, we have Jane Groh from Millersville University discussing the themes of 'hope' and 'despair' in Malory's *Morte d'Arthur*. Then Markus Patterson from the University of Tulsa will be speaking about modern pedagogical methods for teaching Arthurian legend."

Annie looked around at Geoff and Mary Kay, the other historians in the room. Mary Kay rolled her eyes and Geoff just smiled enigmatically, not making eye contact. The hour before Betty presented her paper was going to be a long one.

"Finally," continued the mousy session organizer, "Betty Randall from the University of Michigan will tell us about her recent discovery of a new manuscript which adds to our understanding of the relationship between Arthur and Mordred. Jane?"

The scholar named Jane Groh approached the podium and Annie turned to her laptop, suddenly understanding the real reason why people brought laptops to conference sessions. She opened her internet browser, grateful to Geoff for waving her into the back row.

When it was Betty's turn to present, Annie closed Facebook and Twitter and the Gchat conversation she was having with Gina (She was fine, she was making some friends, and she might actually stay for the dance!) and opened the Word document she meant to take notes on. Then when Betty began to speak, Annie closed her laptop and just listened. So did Geoff.

"For those of you who have been following Arthurian breaking news," Betty began, to the accompaniment of some chuckles by older members of the audience who knew her, "you might already know that I made an extremely exciting discovery last summer in the archives. I submitted a proposal for Kalamazoo, had it accepted, and spent the next six months trying to figure out if my discovery was both real — not a forgery — and new — not previously published in something I should have read already. If one of those outcomes had transpired, I'm afraid I would have had very little to say to you today." More chuckles. "As it turns out, this text is both real and new, and this session marks its first public presentation in modern times."

She hit the button on her presentation clicker and a photo of the manuscript appeared on the screen. Some people in the audience clapped. Annie thought that was a little weird. Mary Kay sat back in her chair and rolled her eyes again. Betty was enjoying this too much. But to be fair, this was essentially the world premier of her manuscript.

"The text is Welsh, and I have it printed here for you on a handout next to my English translation, which I will read now. Please excuse my clunky translation. At this point, I mean for it to be literal rather than poetic." Betty began to read the poem's introduction while the other presenters passed out photocopies of the text and translation to everyone in the room. Annie looked down at hers and followed along with the English as Betty read:

> *Arthur and his men came around the hills*
> *Knowing they were outnumbered by the troops of Mordred*
> *Which poured out from all sides, in the trees, behind the crumbling*
> *   fortresses*
> *Bedivere led the left flank, brave and strong*
> *He looked toward Arthur for the signal, waiting patiently*
> *To confront the adversary as they trickled around the bend*
> *Ruthless Kei on the right eyed the narrow passage*
> *Ready to send forth his troops*
> *One glance from Arthur was all it would take*
> *Gawain held the rear, his sharp eyes looking out*

On all sides

While Arthur, always mindful of fair Guinevere,

Looked straight at Mordred who opposed him

Now! He gave the signal and his troops burst forth

Arthur went right with Kei

While Gawain and the rear guard stormed forth

But Mordred, seeming to neglect the battle,

Chased Arthur off the field and cornered him

In the shell of an old Roman stronghold

You, he accused

But Arthur did not wait for him to speak

He unsheathed his sword and charged

Impaling Mordred on its point while receiving

A similar blow from the enemy sword

The battle endured

And thanks to the skill and bravery

Of Bedivere, Kei, and Gawain, succeeded

In routing Mordred's troops to the far side of the hills

But Arthur and Mordred were nowhere to be found

Finally discovered by Bedivere,

Arthur was rescued and taken to safety, a hero

Mordred lay forgotten

Everyone in the room sat in silence for a moment, staring at their handouts and letting the words sink in. Annie shivered. She couldn't believe how some of the details of this poem complemented her own text. *Mordred lay forgotten.*

It took Annie a moment to realize that Betty had continued talking after reading her translation. "—based on the hand and style probably the eighth or ninth century" she was saying. "The next step will be to carbon date the manuscript. I'll start writing the grant as soon as I get home from Kalamazoo. But if my suspicions about the date are correct, then this will be the oldest text to mention Arthur's encounter with Mordred. Furthermore, it would be the only pre-Galfridian source that explicitly portrays Mordred and Arthur as adversaries."

The ending is strange, too, thought Annie. Arthur was remembered as a hero and Mordred lay forgotten. Annie's text had to do with changing the ways that Mordred and Arthur were remembered after their deaths, and Betty's text contained an early representation of those memories. Annie opened her laptop back up and started typing frantically.

The room cleared out pretty quickly after the session, leaving only people who wanted to talk to Betty. To Annie's (and probably Betty's) great disappointment, the session organizer had requested that the three presenters take questions together at the end, which resulted in an utterly worthless discussion period, so Betty was forced to stay after the session to actually discuss her manuscript. Annie, Marshall, Geoff, and Mary Kay all stayed back, and Annie had a lot to say. This time, she didn't have to muster any courage to converse with big deal scholars. She knew what she had to say was important.

"I definitely see a connection," she said, setting her laptop down on the table in the front of the room where they were all gathered. "This memory stuff." She turned to Mary Kay. "Do any of your texts mention memory? Specifically the memory of Arthur, how people want him to be remembered after his death?"

Mary Kay shook her head. "I don't think so, but I can check. I need to get to the library today to double-check Photius anyway — I might as well look at them all. My paper's tomorrow afternoon and after talking with you guys I think I need to make some changes before I present. There are a lot of connections I didn't see before."

Annie smiled. She was actually contributing to this woman's scholarship.

"And what about the sigils?" Marshall asked. "Where do they fit in?"

"Oh my God, Gavin," Mary Kay whispered. She closed her eyes and brought her hands to her temples. "I knew I was forgetting something."

"I'm surprised you remember anything at all from last night," Betty said acidly.

"No, I need to call Gavin," Mary Kay said, ignoring her. "If he can identify those sigils, then that might suggest a context for Annie's text. Then the connections between your text and Annie's text will become clearer. And possibly my texts, but I'm not sure yet — I have to get to the library. I'll go as soon as I call Gavin. But I think we hit upon a real discovery here, and if that's the case, I'm going to report it all in my talk tomorrow. It'll be some real Arthurian 'breaking news.'" She flashed Betty a winning smile and Betty scowled back.

Annie stifled a laugh. She didn't think Betty appreciated Mary Kay's sense of humor, but Annie was starting to like Mary Kay more and more the more time she spent with her.

"Well?" Betty said after a moment.

Mary Kay stared at her blankly.

"Are you going to call?"

"Oh, yes." Mary Kay dug in her bag for a moment before unearthing a heavily Otterboxed smart phone and scrolling through her contacts for Gavin Chen. "Hello, Gavin?" she said into the phone after a moment.

"Come on, Mary Kay, put it on speaker!" Betty exclaimed in a higher voice than usual. The others all stared back at her, but Mary Kay obliged.

"—a little early for a Kalamazoo drunk dial, isn't it?" came a male voice over the speaker phone.

"Yeah, but a little late for a 'get your ass up here — you're needed' call. I should have made that yesterday," Mary Kay replied.

"This was supposed to be my year off," said Gavin.

"Well you picked the wrong year, buddy. Betty and I, and this grad student of Murray Penge's, made some pretty interesting discoveries about King Arthur this weekend, but we need a material culture person to help out. You see, this text that Annie — that's the grad student — brought to our attention has these symbols on it, and none of us can identify them."

"The lost sigils of King Arthur?" Gavin asked. His voice sounded awed.

"Yes!" shouted Marshall. "Someone else knows what I'm talking about!"

"Who's that?" asked Gavin. "Am I on speaker?"

"Hi Gavin — it's me!" Betty said before she could stop herself. Everyone ignored her.

"That is interesting," said Gavin. "I would like to see them."

"So you'll come up?" asked Mary Kay.

"No. Maybe. Just — could someone email me a picture so I could take a look?"

Without a word, Annie turned to her laptop and started composing an email.

"I'm just gavinchen@nd.edu."

Annie nodded and attached some photos. She looked around the room — everyone was grinning like Marshall. Finally she would have some answers about the strange images. And maybe, if Mary Kay's suspicions were correct, they would all have some answers about who King Arthur really was.

| 9 |

Camlann

Wales, 537

The right flank of Arthur's army launched their spears and Mordred kicked his horse and veered left. His army made the first move and had the advantage. Mordred was going after Arthur.

He rode behind his infantry guard and sought out a crumbling Roman tower. But Arthur saw him and for a moment they locked eyes. It was too late for Mordred to turn his horse around, so he continued on to the tower. Arthur went there too. They were going to confront each other head-on.

On the far side of the Roman tower, out of view of the battle that raged between the hills, Arthur did not wait for Mordred to speak. He unsheathed his sword and charged. But Mordred was ready — he pulled out his sword, too, and Mordred felt it enter Arthur's flesh as he was knocked from his horse, impaled on Arthur's sword.

The pain was so great, Mordred could not stay conscious. He heard his horse shriek in pain, but nothing could be done. He saw Arthur's men — Bedivere and that braggart Kei, and the wimpy one, Gawain. Then Arthur was gone, and he was alone, dying.

A flash of light, and an angel appeared before his eyes. He had the appearance of an old man with along white beard, and he wore robes of the deepest blue glinting with stars. It took Mordred a few moments to realize that this was not an angel, it was Merlin the magician. He must not be dead after all.

Merlin muttered an incantation while smearing some magical ointment over Mordred's wound and pulled him on to the back of his horse. They rode through the night to Merlin's retreat where his servant girl tended Mordred's wound properly. Mordred was fed and bathed and resting by the fire when Merlin spoke to him. His voice was quiet, thoughtful. "Did your fighting accomplish what you wanted it to?" he asked.

"Arthur is dead?" Mordred countered. "I stabbed him with my sword."

The old wizard shook his head slowly. "Not dead, but fatally wounded. He will not appear in battle again."

Mordred's eyes lit up for a brief moment. He had finally defeated his biggest adversary. But the answer to Merlin's question had to be "no." He was not satisfied. Arthur would die a hero while Mordred was left to die alone. Everyone would remember that it was Arthur who defeated Mordred, even though it was his last battle. The Battle of Camlann did *not* accomplish what Mordred wanted it to. But he could not say that to Merlin. Not Merlin who saved him. Merlin who was always on Arthur's side. But with Merlin's help, he *could* accomplish what he set out to from the beginning.

"Yes," Mordred answered finally. "I have defeated Arthur. He will not fight another battle."

Merlin nodded slowly, a hint of a smile appearing at the corners of his mouth.

"There's just one more thing I want to do, before I die myself." He looked down at his bandaged chest. It hurt to move. "I want to write a spell. C-can you help me write a spell to ensure that people will remember me at the Battle of Camlann?"

Merlin took a seat beside Mordred, by the fire. "A memory spell. Those are highly complex. You will need an object."

"What sort of object?" Mordred asked.

"Oh, anything that can be passed on to other people, and survive a long time. Parchment, perhaps?" Merlin waved his hand and Mordred caught sight of a length of clean parchment floating leisurely towards them from the writing table in the corner. "I could put a spell on this parchment so that the memories it contains will take hold over all of society once someone else reads it. You will have to write the words, though." At this, Merlin stared pointedly at Mordred, his eyes seeming to stare straight into Mordred's soul. "The spell will be yours."

Mordred reached out his hand to take the parchment and nodded, unsure of what to say.

Now Merlin stood and stoked the fire. "It would also help to include your token, if you have one. Some sign or symbol that represents you. If it is *you* that you want people to remember."

Mordred shivered at his last comment. It was as if Merlin knew he didn't want the spell to be about himself. It was as if Merlin was capable of that darkest, most powerful magical art, seeing into the minds of others.

"Now it is time for an old man to get some rest," Merlin said finally, once he had finished with the fire. "You should sleep too. It will help you heal. When I see you in the morning, I will take your parchment with your spell on it and I will say the words that will ensure its contents take hold in the memories of many."

"Thank you, Merlin," Mordred replied.

Without another word, Merlin disappeared through a door into the other room in the house. The servant girl nodded at Mordred and lay down in her cot on the other side of the room. Mordred waited for her to fall asleep before stealing away to Merlin's writing desk where he sat down and wrote in Latin words around the edges of the entire page: *Memoriam Arturi contemnamus; non heros, sed homicida; mille gentes occidebat saevus Arturius; non Mordredus conservare potest.*

He smiled down at the words when he was finished. Now for the sign. He reached into his tunic and pulled out the piece of cloth he wore close to himself in battle. That he wore close to himself always. It was a ripped piece of a cape that once belonged to Arthur bearing Arthur's insignia. Mordred couldn't believe his luck. When he had stolen the garment ages ago, when he first found out who Arthur was, when he realized that Arthur had to die, he hadn't realized that this very memento would be the sign of Arthur's downfall. Slowly, being careful not to make a single line go amiss, Mordred copied the image in the center of his spell. All that was left to add was the magic, and for that he needed a magician.

"Merlin can't see this," Mordred whispered aloud. He might have been able to hide the text from Merlin long enough for the wizard to say the words, but not the insignia. Merlin would recognize the symbol of Arthur from across the room. The risk was too great. He needed to find someone else to put the magic in his spell. He spit into the fire. He supposed he had known all along that he would need Morgan in the end, but he still did not like the idea of consorting with an evil like her.

Resigning himself to his new plan, Mordred folded the parchment in half and stashed it safely inside his bag. Planning to set out the moment he awoke, he put the bag under his head into something of a pillow, lay down, and fell into a dreamless sleep.

| 10 |

Friend Dates

Kalamazoo, 2017

Annie decided to skip the wine hour and head straight to the Valley Dining Hall around six for dinner. Lunch hadn't been too bad, and Annie actually kind of enjoyed eating by herself. She never made it into the dining hall, however.

Just as she got to the bottom of the hill, she saw Geoff walking toward her, away from Valley Three. He was alone. "Hey Annie. Headed to dinner?" he asked casually.

"Yeah," Annie said. "Want to join?" she asked before she could stop herself.

Geoff stopped. "Dining hall?" He considered it a moment, and then said, "Would you rather go somewhere more exciting?"

"Like the British Empire?" asked Annie, naming the only Kalamazoo establishment she knew.

Geoff smiled and Annie felt her cheeks go warm. God, I look like such an amateur, Annie thought. He can probably tell I've never even been to a conference before. "How about Bell's?" Geoff suggested.

"Bell's?"

"Like Two Hearted? Oberon?"

Beers. "There's a beer-themed restaurant in Kalamazoo?"

"It's the brewery, silly! Where they make those beers. You like Bell's?"

"Yeah, I do," Annie replied, looking down at Geoff's brown leather shoes instead of at Geoff. Her heart started beating faster. "I don't know if I want to go out, though. I was kind of thinking I'd just have a quick dinner in the dining hall and then turn in early and read. Today was kind of an exhausting day." She didn't mention her early breakfast, remembering how she blew him off for the keynote that morning. It seemed like it was a lifetime ago.

"Aww, come on," Geoff pleaded. "Just a quick dinner. You haven't really been to Kalamazoo until you go to Bell's."

Annie looked up and saw Geoff smile. He was smiling with his eyes again, completely unlike Chad. "All right," Annie said, smiling back. "Just a quick dinner."

"Great! My rental car's just back here in the Valley Three parking lot. Mind if I drive?"

"Go ahead," Annie said, grateful to not have to lose her parking space in Valley One. "Thanks."

Bell's was in a huge old warehouse packed with medievalists still wearing their name badges. Annie realized she was still wearing hers too and quickly stuffed it in her bag. As soon as she and Geoff got to their table, she took off Gina's blazer and straightened out the green dress, wishing she had thought to change before dinner.

"Uncomfortable conference clothes?" Geoff asked.

"They're my roommate's," Annie admitted. "I don't really have any professional clothes."

"That's the great thing about Kalamazoo, Jamie was telling me. It's not like other conferences were you feel like you have to wear a suit, or something equivalent to one. It's mostly just about being a medievalist in whatever way you're comfortable. People dress comfortably too." Geoff gestured to his own dark blue cable knit sweater and straight leg jeans, and then around the room at all the other medievalists. He was right — none of them was wearing a suit.

"Thanks for the tip," Annie said, looking back down at her own outfit that was the opposite of comfortable. "I'll have to remember that for next year."

"You're coming back next year?"

Annie smiled. Geoff caught her, and he looked delighted about it. "I like Kalamazoo. I think I will come back next year."

"Great — I'll definitely know someone here then. Can I get you a drink?"

"Sure," said Annie. "Two Hearted."

"Coming right up!"

Geoff disappeared in search of the counter while Annie stayed behind at the table, wondering what to make of this dinner with Geoff. Was this a date? She didn't want to be on a date, but she didn't mind having dinner one-on-one with Geoff either, and she wasn't sure how she felt about that yet.

Geoff was good company. He made Annie feel comfortable. He talked so naturally, and Annie found it easy to talk back to him. She tried to remember her early dates with Chadwick from her freshman year of college, the last time she dated someone new. It was a long time ago, but she couldn't remember Chad ever making her feel like this. With Chad, dates were an adventure. They were something new with someone unpredictable and dangerous. He had said he cared about Annie and would never let anything bad happen to her. And he was right, sort of. Nothing bad *happened* happened, but Annie never really felt that Chad cared about her. He was always doing things that he wanted to do and saying he was doing them for her. But half the time she didn't feel comfortable doing them.

Annie shook her head vigorously, hoping none of the medievalists around could see this strange mannerism — none of them were looking. She had to get Chad out of her head. Replace him with Geoff, she thought. Rebound. Rebound three years late. She barely knew Geoff, but every interaction with him, every time he made a suggestion, he always seemed like he would be okay with whatever answer Annie gave.

Geoff returned to the table with two pints of Two Hearted and two menus. Annie reached into her bag for her wallet but Geoff put his hand up. "This is my treat. I'm the one who dragged you away from the dining hall and brought you to a real restaurant."

"I feel like I should pay," said Annie. "It's not like this is a date."

"It doesn't have to be a date," said Geoff.

Annie looked up from her beer, surprised.

"I'm sorry. I shouldn't have presumed." Geoff set down his beer and looked seriously at Annie. "This doesn't have to be a date, just a dinner between new friends. That is, if you want to be friends. But I would be lying if I said I didn't like you, in a romantic kind of way. Ever since dinner yesterday you've intrigued me." He shrugged. Casually. "I feel like I want to know more."

"What's that supposed to mean?"

"You know, get to know you, that's all. But if you're not interested, or if you already have a partner, I totally understand, and that doesn't make me not want to get to know you anymore. Just as friends, then."

Annie nodded, perhaps a bit too vigorously. She was still trying to get the Chad out. "Just as friends."

"All right," agreed Geoff. "This isn't a date. We're just two new early medieval historian friends getting to know one another. That's like the primary purpose of Kalamazoo anyway."

Annie breathed a sigh of relief. She felt her shoulders start to relax — she hadn't even noticed they were tense. After a pause, she held up her beer to Geoff's. "Friend dates?"

Geoff held up his and clinked it into Annie's. "Friend dates."

Then Annie proceeded to have a completely normal dinner with a friend, like she wasn't even at a conference at all. Over the next two hours, they just talked and talked without ever running out of things to say. After they got their dinner, they even started talking about things that had nothing to do with King Arthur or medieval studies or Kalamazoo or grad school.

Annie learned that Geoff was from Philadelphia and that he was a really good soccer player and had played in college. He had two older sisters who each had two little kids and he loved going home for Christmas and over the summer to play with them. He said his one nephew was going to be a better soccer player than he was. He also had two younger brothers, one of whom worked on computers and the other who was in the military.

Then Annie told Geoff a little bit about her home in Northern Michigan where her parents — a car mechanic and a librarian — lived the dream of doing all the outdoor activities. She didn't tell him that she didn't share her parents' passion for camping and hunting and swimming in lakes. He seemed so interested in her idyllic description of a midwest full of old hippies inhabiting lakeside cottages and she didn't want to spoil it.

Geoff told Annie all about how much he had loved college and his classes and professors and that was what made him want to become a professor himself. "I just knew I needed to be there, in a university, helping out students like myself. Telling them, 'It's okay. It may be hard, but you've got this!" These words accompanied a smile so warm and genuine that Annie felt like he was saying them directly to her, and not to imaginary undergrads Geoff hoped to mentor one day.

Annie didn't feel like telling Geoff about her undergraduate years, mostly because she spent all four of them in a relationship she was trying to forget. But she did tell him why she wanted to become a professor, or at least a historian.

"I always knew," she said, the sides of her mouth twitching upward in an involuntary smile. "I could tell when I was in high school when my teacher taught us about Eleanor of Aquitaine that I wanted to learn more about the middle ages. When I got to college, I immediately tried to declare a history major, but they made us wait until sophomore year to declare anything."

"I bet you still declared history, though, right?" asked Geoff.

Annie nodded and continued her story. She didn't really like sharing personal stories in general, but this was one she loved to tell. "I got to take one history class my first semester, though, and I chose History of Russia One. I think it was the only pre-modern class that fit in my schedule. I didn't know anything about Russia at the time. The class turned out to be awesome, though, and so did the professor."

Geoff just smiled when Annie paused to take a sip of her beer.

"I wrote a paper for that class," she continued, "which was really difficult, but I worked super hard on it and I was pretty sure I had done well. Then one day, during finals week but before we got our papers back, I was standing at the circulation desk of the library trying to negotiate with the librarian to waive my fines." She smirked and Geoff laughed along. "Then Professor Goldfrank out of nowhere came up behind me. He said, 'Hey! Did you know you got an A on your paper?' 'I did?' I said. 'Yeah,' he said, 'it was really good, a pleasure to read, really smart. You can really think through this stuff, you know?' 'Well,' I said to him, 'that's good to hear, because I think I want to be a historian.' 'You want to get a PhD in history?' Goldfrank asked me. I thought that was part of being a historian, so I nodded. 'I can't believe that!' said Goldfrank. He was so happy. 'You want to get a PhD in history!' Then the librarian, standing there awkwardly during this whole exchange, waived my fines, and here I am!"

"So you just love history so much," said Geoff.

Annie looked up, smiling a little more. "I guess I do. I haven't thought much about the 'professor' part, honestly. I don't have much teaching experience yet, and I'm not really committed to doing that anyway. But whatever job I get after the PhD, I just want to be a historian."

"That's awesome," said Geoff. "I guess I came to history in a similar way — just knowing. I was at college for soccer and just planning on doing the whole liberal arts curriculum and deciding what I wanted to be later on. Then I took this upper-level seminar on the medieval Mediterranean as a sophomore — I don't know what I was thinking — but I realized that late antiquity was *just like now*. Entire neighborhoods in Philadelphia are just falling apart, and sometimes people steamroll in and gentrify, but that doesn't always happens. Sometimes the hundred-year-old buildings are restored and made even better. Sometimes crumbled buildings are taken down and the land is repurposed as a park or a garden. Old churches that closed in the '90s became mosques or community centers. The early middle ages aren't *less* than the Roman empire, they're just *different*, and I love it."

"I love it, too," Annie said. "And I haven't thought about it like that before, but now I always will."

"I didn't mean to blow your mind or anything," Geoff joked. "But I've thought about it a lot. A lot of people ask me why I study medieval history, because they think we're supposed to do me-search or something. Which is bullshit — me-search can be so limiting. But the 'me' in medieval history is exactly what I just told you."

Now it was Annie's turn to say, "That's amazing." She wasn't sure she had found her "me" in medieval history.

After dinner, Geoff drove Annie back to Valley Three. In their non-stop conversation that continued all the way back to the dorms, she had forgotten to tell him she wanted to be dropped off at Valley One. When they got out of the car, Geoff asked her if she wanted to go inside in for the reception.

"What reception?" Annie asked.

"All the free beer in Valley Three?"

"They do that every night?" Annie asked. What kind of a conference was this?

"Just Thursday and Friday," said Geoff. "Tomorrow night's the dance, and you have to pay for drinks there, which is why a lot of people just bring liquor to the dorms and pregame. I have a water bottle half-full of Jameson in my room right now, which makes me feel like I'm in high school all over again, except in high school it wasn't Jameson. Anyway, you are going to the dance tomorrow, right?"

"Probably," Annie answered. "Maybe. I haven't decided yet."

"Well if you do decide, maybe we can go together. The only other person I really know here is Jamie, and that just feels kind of weird."

"I'll think about it," Annie said. She looked over at the far porch of Valley Three, like it was last night and she was checking for Mary Kay. Then she turned back to Geoff. "I'm tired now, though. You enjoy the reception. I'm going to head back up to Valley One and call it a night."

"Sounds good. I'll see you tomorrow, Annie."

Geoff turned to walk inside the door but Annie called out, "Hey wait!"

"Yes?"

"Do you want to meet for breakfast tomorrow morning?" she asked.

"Sure," Geoff answered, his eyes lighting up. "What time did you have in mind? Do you want to see the keynote?"

Annie crinkled her nose. "No. Do you?"

"No," said Geoff. "How about we sleep in a little and meet at the Valley Dining Hall at nine?"

"It's a date," replied Annie.

Geoff raised his eyebrows. "A date?"

"A *friend* date."

Geoff went inside and Annie walked back down to the street that led to the other Valleys. As she passed the first entrance to Valley Three, her eyes scanned the porch again, not realizing she was looking for Mary Kay until Mary Kay herself waved her over and shouted, "Annie Fisher? Is that you?"

"Yeah!" Annie shouted back.

"Come on up! Have a drink with us!"

Annie hesitated and then summoned Geoff's courage as she started up the stairs. Mary Kay was with her two late antique historian friends from the night before. This time they were all leaning against the railing while other people occupied the picnic table.

"Hi Mary Kay," Annie said, nodding awkwardly to the two men. "I'm actually on my way to bed, but I'll come say hi for a few minutes." Annie leaned against the railing as well, trying to look comfortable. She was glad that Mary Kay had no idea how difficult it was for her to join three professors on a porch at a social event without any other grad students around to back her up.

"Do you want to go inside and get a drink?" Mary Kay offered.

"No thanks. I just had two Two Hearteds."

Mary Kay nodded. "I'm taking it easy tonight too. So," she continued, lowering her voice a little, "have you checked your email since this afternoon?"

Annie shook her head. She had checked it before dinner but didn't see anything that Mary Kay would be interested in. She hadn't looked at all since she met Geoff, though.

"Check it," Mary Kay said. "Not now!" she exclaimed when Annie reached in her bag for her phone. "I mean when you get back to your room. I'll spoil it now, though — Gavin *really* liked your photos."

"Really?" Annie asked excitedly. She had almost forgotten she sent photos of the sigils to a random archaeologist named Gavin that afternoon. "And?" she asked.

Mary Kay looked at her watch. "And he should be getting to Kalamazoo in about an hour or so. I don't think he'll come out tonight, but you'll have to meet him tomorrow. He's a trip. And he recognized your symbols. Turns out he found some very similar images on a dig in Wales last summer. He didn't know what to make of them and has just been sitting on the photos, but as soon as he saw yours he practically shit his pants."

Annie's jaw dropped. "That's what he said?"

"Well, he didn't say 'shit his pants,' but he did say he recognized the symbols and thinks he can situate them in west Wales, so that's something."

"Did you make it to the library today?" Annie asked, remembering Mary Kay was thinking through some discoveries of her own.

"I did, as a matter of fact, but I'm still trying to work some stuff out. I want to talk to Gavin before I draw any conclusions. But I have a feeling tomorrow will be a lot of me rewriting my paper with you and Gavin and Betty before I present. Like I said earlier, I think this is a big discovery, and we're all working on it together.

I'll just present it tomorrow afternoon. But it isn't really my paper anymore."

"You really mean that?" Annie asked.

"Of course! I'm not going to take credit for all the work the rest of you have done! Especially not the Welsh poetry — definitely not that."

"But I mean, me," said Annie. "Do you really think I'm contributing to your discovery?"

Mary Kay looked seriously at Annie. "You more than anyone, Annie," she said. "Don't discount yourself, ever. And *especially* don't discount yourself because you're a grad student. You're here, aren't you? You're a real medievalist. You're just as real as me or Betty or Gavin."

"You really think so?"

Mary Kay laughed. "Please. I wouldn't be wasting my time if it weren't true."

For some reason, that callous statement comforted Annie more than her words of comfort did. Mary Kay took her seriously as a colleague, she realized. Mary Kay McKinley — this big deal scholar whom Geoff wanted to be when he grew up — thought of Annie as a colleague.

"Okay," Annie said, smiling. "I believe you. But I really have to get back and get to bed, especially now I know I have an exciting email from Gavin waiting for me."

"Of course — I won't keep you," said Mary Kay. "But first, what's your phone number? I want to have it in case I need to get in contact with you tomorrow before my paper."

Grinning, Annie reached back into her bag for her phone. That sealed it. Annie had another new friend in academia. A new, well-known, published, *grownup* friend in academia.

| 11 |

Collaboration

Annie woke up before the alarm on her phone went off, feeling refreshed. She pulled the sad little Kalamazoo blanket up over her shoulders and turned onto her side, a smile stretching over her face. The dorm bed wasn't so bad after all.

Annie took longer than usual to pick out her outfit that morning, despite only having packed a few things. She had plenty of time to get ready, though. It was eight-thirty and she wasn't meeting the guys until nine. (She had texted Marshall the night before and invited him to breakfast too. She didn't want him to feel left out after he went out of his way to include her at dinner their first night.)

Annie pulled on her jeans and Doc Martens and the orange sweater Gina had unearthed from the back of her closet, unaware that she was dressing in something she was comfortable in rather than an outfit she thought was conference-worthy. She suddenly realized this with the sweater half over her head and paused to consider whether it was "professional" enough to dress like this. She thought of Geoff and how comfortable he looked the night before, and how professional he looked when he talked about his interests, and decided that confidence looked professional. Now if only she could muster up some confidence...

Geoff was waiting for her when she arrived at the Valley Dining Hall. So was Marshall, but on the other side of the doorway.

"Morning, Annie," Geoff said. "You look really nice today. Like you slept well."

"I did," replied Annie. "The dorm beds are better the second night."

"Agreed," said Marshall, skipping forward to join Annie and Geoff. "Shall we?"

Marshall led the way into the dining hall and Annie immediately regretted inviting him to breakfast. There was a tension that wasn't present when she was just hanging out with Geoff. If Geoff didn't want Marshall at breakfast, though, he didn't show it. The two of them talked at length about the other papers they'd seen the day before. Annie asked a few questions, but she was mostly silent, eating her eggs and toast. She hadn't been to any other sessions besides Betty's. (She guessed that made her a bad conference-goer.)

After awhile, Marshall turned to Annie and asked, "What did you end up doing for dinner last night? I looked for you at the wine hour but I didn't see you."

"I skipped the wine hour," Annie replied. "I told you the other day — I don't think Franzia is worth it at all. Then I went to Bell's with Geoff." Annie's eyes briefly met Geoff's and lingered for a split-second before she looked away.

"Oh," said Marshall.

"What did you do for dinner?" Annie asked.

Marshall shrugged. His shrug didn't look anything like Geoff's. "I texted some English department folks and had dinner with them."

"That's nice. Oh — hey!" Annie said, remembering something she wanted to tell Marshall. "I ran into Mary Kay last night, at the reception in Valley Three."

"You went to the Valley Three reception?" This time it was Geoff asking the question.

"Not really. Just on my way back to my room I saw Mary Kay on the porch and she waved me over." Geoff and Marshall nodded and Annie continued. "Anyway, she told me that Gavin Chen, that archaeologist the professors were all talking about yesterday, identified the sigils from my photos — he found those exact images on a dig in Wales last summer!"

Marshall almost spit out his food. "Holy shit, they *are* real," he mumbled.

"She said Gavin was driving up to Kalamazoo right then. He should be here now. He'll be at Mary Kay's paper and we can talk to him."

"I can't believe it," Marshall said, awestruck.

"I know, this really is fantastic," said Geoff. He was flipping through his program. "There was a late antique ethnicity panel I wanted to go to at 3:30, but now I'm checking to see if it really is that important so I can go to Mary Kay's instead. I hate that they put two late antiquity sessions side by side at Kalamazoo. There are like ten of us — can't they make it so we can all go to each other's papers?"

"I don't care what else I had planned for 3:30," Marshall said. "I'm *definitely* going to that session."

"Me too, obviously," said Annie. She looked down at her phone that was sitting face up beside her plate rather than in her bag. She kept it nearby all morning, secretly hoping for a call from Mary Kay. To her surprise, there was a text message waiting for her. She turned on the screen and smiled. The text was from Mary Kay.

Can you come to Fetzer as soon as you're up? Gavin and Betty are here and we're working on paper. Text when you're here and I'll tell you what room we're in.

"Hey," Annie said, looking up at the two guys. They both had stopped eating to watch Annie check her message. "Gavin and Betty and Mary Kay are working in Fetzer and they want us to come too. Do you know where that is?"

"Yep — just follow me," Geoff said, picking up his empty plate.

"I can't believe it," Marshall said again. He was in shock. Annie wasn't surprised — the sigils had been the most interesting part of the project from the beginning for him. She wondered whether he would faint when he met Gavin.

"Just a second," said Annie, still smiling at her phone. She had just replied to Mary Kay's message and wanted to revel in the moment a little more. "I need to finish my breakfast."

The Fetzer center was already full of conference-goers getting ready to attend the ten o'clock sessions when Annie, Marshall, and Geoff arrived. They went upstairs and found the classroom that Mary Kay told Annie to meet her in. Annie ignored the sign that said "Lactation Room" and pushed open the door. Once the guys were sure the room was not occupied by someone using a breast pump, they followed behind Annie.

Mary Kay was leaning against a desk frowning at an enormous MacBook Pro. She looked amazing in a gray pantsuit and Annie made a mental note to complement her later that day. Annie thought she should start developing a professional style that looked more like Mary Kay than Gina. Or Betty, who wore a paisley scarf over a black knit sweater-dress.

Betty was hovering over the laptop on the other side of the desk, a little too close to an older Asian man wearing a bright blue sport coat with khakis. She kept shifting her weight and glancing over at the man — Gavin — every couple of seconds. When the grad students entered the room she called out, "Oh good, you're here. Did you bring your laptop?"

"No, I just came from breakfast," Annie said. "But he has my photos." She gestured with her chin toward the big laptop that was currently displaying photos of ancient rocks that must be from Gavin's dig.

Mary Kay turned around and stepped toward Annie. Annie noticed that she wore a floral printed dress shirt under the suit jacket and practically swooned. "Annie, this is Gavin Chen," she said, "professor of Archaeology at Notre Dame. And this," she said, flinging her hand out toward the laptop, "is his evidence. Take a closer look at those rocks, Annie — those are unmistakably your symbols." Marshall pushed past Annie to look at the images.

Gavin Chen took a step toward Annie as well and put out his hand for her to shake. Annie shook his hand firmly, thinking that she really was getting better at this and maybe she could handle the networking aspect of conferences after all. "It's a pleasure to meet you, Annie," Gavin said. "Those codex pages you have there are really something special. The Latin inscription beside the scribbles helps puts the sigils in context. I think they do have something to do with Arthur. Perhaps they strengthen the spell by making it specific to him. I'll need to look into it further."

"And," Betty chimed in, "thanks to the references that Mary Kay has been studying, especially the one she looked up yesterday, we know these signs have something to do with a warlord wreaking havoc in England, who sounds suspiciously like the Arthur in my poem." She bounced over to Gavin but stopped just shy of him and froze. She was behaving more strangely than normal, Annie thought, and that was saying something.

Mary Kay looked up from her own, much smaller laptop. "Annie, this is huge. References in Jordanes, Venantius Fortunatus, and a sixth-century author quoted by Photius all speak of a criminal warlord surfacing in Britain in the early sixth century. The Photius source actually mentions that the warlord engraved signs in the earth. Apparently he was in the midst of a huge campaign to wipe out all the Germans and Romans from Britain and restore it to some sort of purely Celtic state. Gavin found these signs inscribed in strategic locations throughout Wales and western England. They seem to be apotropaic devices designed to keep out people whom Arthur had already defeated. By the looks of Gavin's findings, it seems like he got pretty far — and killed a lot of people in the process. Some of the inscriptions are quite monumental. Then Mordred was trying to save them. He opposed Arthur, but not because he was jealous or wanted his throne or whatever the later legends tell us. He was trying to stop Arthur from wiping out the population of Britain. And, as we learned from Betty's poem, he succeeded, but was left for dead by Arthur's cruel underlings and forgotten, until he was remembered only as a villain."

She let out a deep sigh and held out her hands. "Annie. This changes everything."

Annie let out her breath, too. She hadn't realized she was holding it. "Whoa," she mouthed. Mary Kay was extremely sharp when she wasn't hungover. "Are you sure?" Annie asked after a moment's silence.

Mary Kay put her hands up again, but Betty and Gavin were nodding vigorously.

"The argument is practically water-tight," Betty said. "When you put all our evidence together. It all makes sense."

"Except —" started Gavin.

Everyone turned to look at him. Betty furrowed her eyebrows dramatically and put one hand on her hip.

"Except we don't know if the codex is authentic," he said. He turned back to his laptop and opened up another file. Annie recognized her own photo of the centerfold of her grimoire that featured the two sigils of King Arthur inside the Latin words: *Memoriam Ar-*

turi contemnamus; non heros, sed homicida; mille gentes occidebat saevus Arturius; non Mordredus conservare potest.

Annie felt her cheeks get hot and started to turn away. Marshall and Geoff both took a protective step toward her. Everything hinged on her. Perhaps the discovery hinged on her, and that was cool, but so did its verification. And she dropped the ball and didn't bring the manuscript to the conference. How could she be so unprepared?

"But that's not relevant *today*," Betty snapped, seeing the look on Annie's face. "That's why I've been writing this grant over here." She gestured to the third laptop on the table. "What do you think I've been typing the entire time? I already gave *my* paper yesterday, which you would know if you had been here." She glared at Gavin. "Mary Kay is presenting all our discoveries at *her* session, and meanwhile, I'm applying for money to have the parchment carbon dated so we can get closer to verifying its authenticity."

"And I'm going to say all that in my presentation today," Mary Kay said, specifically to Annie. "Even if you had the pages with you today and we could analyze them materially, we still couldn't get a scientific read on the ink or the parchment for another couple of months at least."

Annie started to feel a little better, but Gavin was still scowling. "I would just be more comfortable if we could have those codex pages here with us." He was rubbing his fingers and thumb together like he had an imaginary piece of parchment between them.

Betty swatted Gavin with the back of her hand and then quickly recoiled. "Don't be such a pill, Gavin," she said, laughing nervously.

Gavin glanced up at Betty out of the corner of his eye and Annie instinctively turned to look at Geoff, who gave a fleeting smile and turned back to Mary Kay.

"Anyway, that's where we're at." Mary Kay had taken a seat at the desk and resumed typing on her laptop while chewing her lip.

Just then, the door opened and a young woman carrying a gigantic tote bag came into the room. She stopped in her tracks when she saw six people spread out in the lactation room. "Um, is this the —" she started to laugh.

"Jesus Christ, we're so sorry!" Betty exclaimed, leaping up from her chair and grabbing up her laptop in a single motion. "Come on, let's get out of here. I told you you couldn't abuse the lactation room even if you did use it for its intended purpose back in the day."

"It wasn't *that* long ago," Mary Kay grumbled, scooping up her own laptop and all her papers that were scattered over the desk. "We'll be out of your way in just a moment," she said.

"No problem," the younger woman replied. She seemed more startled than annoyed. She had already begun setting up her pump before Gavin had a chance to pack up his computer.

"Come on, everybody," Betty said again. "There's a session going on now and the Fetzer foyer will be empty. Let's continue this activity downstairs."

| 12 |

Arthurian Breaking News

Downstairs in the Fetzer lobby, Mary Kay took charge. Recognizing that they had a limited amount of time to finish their presentation, and that their argument needed to be as tight as possible for maximum impact, she was knuckling down, completely serious and as sharp as could be. The news that King Arthur was actually a destructive warlord bent on genocide and Mordred was trying to stop him was groundbreaking, and they only had one chance to get it right.

"Gavin, can you get to the library and find out as much as you can about sigils like this being used as spells? I can incorporate your argument into the talk if you have it to me by lunch."

Gavin nodded his head down once. "Got it. I know exactly where to look."

Mary Kay nodded in imitation. "Good. You — Betty's student —" she barked, pointing at Marshall, "go with him. You seem to know a lot about the images in Annie's manuscript."

"Okay," Marshall said. He looked back at Annie and raised his eyebrows before following Gavin outside. Annie shrugged and turned back to Mary Kay, awaiting her instructions.

"Betty, young people — I need you on social media."

"You know I don't do social media," said Betty.

"But you have friends who are like Twitter royalty."

Betty stared at Mary Kay blankly.

"Lyndsay? Nora Jean?"

"They're on Twitter?" Betty asked. Annie laughed out loud. Even she followed Lyndsay Solomon and Nora Jean Downey, but she hadn't realized they were real-life friends with Betty.

Mary Kay rolled her eyes. "Find them, tell them what we're up to, and get them to hype our session on Twitter. See if one of them can volunteer to live-Tweet, or at least to re-Tweet the Tweets coming from these two." Now she turned to face Annie and Geoff. "You guys have Twitter, don't you?"

They both nodded.

"Good. You start hyping it too. I'm sure you have some grad student followers, and early medieval followers. I'm also going to Tweet a little too to get a late antique audience and then tell them to follow the hashtag since I won't be able to Tweet during my presentation. I will need you two to actually live-Tweet the paper and the question and answer session. Can you do that?"

"Definitely," said Geoff.

"Yeah," said Annie. "What's the hashtag?"

Mary Kay smirked and looked up at Betty, who was smiling back at her. They were on the same page, for once. "Arthurian Breaking News," they said together.

"Got it," Annie replied, grinning.

"Great," said Mary Kay, back to business. "Then, Betty, once you've found your friends and convinced them of their Twitterly mission, I need you to get back to work on the grant. The sooner that's in, the better. I want whoever it is at Oxford reviewing your application to do so with today's Tweetstorm fresh in their mind."

"Christ, Mary Kay, you don't mess around," said Betty. Annie understood that as agreement. So did Mary Kay.

"Perfect. Can I meet everybody back here after lunch? I should have incorporated Gavin's new research by then and we should just be going over everything, making sure I have all the details in the right order — properly attributed, of course." She winked at Annie and Annie tried to pretend Betty or Geoff didn't notice. "Once the presentation's all prepped and ready to go, we'll have a look at Twitter to see what kind of damage Norge and Lyndsay have unleashed, and then we'll haul ass to the presentation room to make sure you all get good seats." She took a deep breath and sat down in an armchair and opened her laptop, crossing her gray pant-suited legs. That was the end of her instructions.

"Come on, guys," Betty urged. "Let's get out of here before she starts breathing fire."

"Does she also run marathons?" Annie asked Betty.

"I think so."

"No," Mary Kay replied without looking up from her laptop. "I've done a few 10Ks but I love my joints too much to do anything longer."

Betty shrugged and led the way outside.

"What do we do now?" Annie asked her once they stepped outside the Fetzer building into the blinding sunlight.

Betty took off her glasses and replaced them with a pair of huge prescription aviators before replying, "Tweet?"

Annie looked at her watch. "The session's not for another five hours — we can't tweet for that long."

"Well I need to find Lyndsay and Norge," Betty answered, exasperated. "Which is going to be impossible — they're probably in a session and there's no cell reception in any of the classrooms here. I'm going to have to leave messages and hope they find me in time."

"Well we should start hyping the session, like Mary Kay said," said Geoff, "but then I think we just go to sessions too. What did you have planned for the 10:30 and 1:30 times?" he asked Annie.

"Nothing, really." In truth, Annie hadn't even looked at the program for Saturday at all.

"Well you can tag along with me, then, if you want," said Geoff, smiling. "I think you'll be interested in the sessions I'm going to anyway."

"All right, I guess I could do that ," Annie replied.

"Oookay, you two," said Betty, looking wistfully over at the library. "I'll see you back here after lunch."

Things were much calmer when Annie and Geoff met back up with the professors and Marshall in Fetzer after lunch. Mary Kay was still staring fixedly at her laptop, but she was much less intense than she had been that morning. Betty seemed to have finished her grant application and was hovering awkwardly as Gavin and Marshall carried on a lively conversation about the sigils, which were displayed on Gavin's laptop.

"How's the presentation coming?" Annie asked, plopping down on an armchair. She was exhausted from the morning session. The papers and discussion were interesting, but she couldn't imagine sitting in multiple sessions a day for an entire weekend. Maybe it was an acquired skill and she would get better with practice.

"Fantastic," replied Mary Kay. "We're basically done, and with time to spare." She turned toward Annie and sighed. "I love that orange sweater Annie — did you have it on earlier?

"Yes," Annie said. "It's okay. You were busy this morning."

"Now you should get something to eat, Mary Kay," Betty interjected. "You want to be at your best for the presentation."

"I can go grab us some food if you like," said Gavin. "Marshall and I haven't eaten either." He turned toward Annie and Geoff.

"Would you like something? My car's right out here — I think I'm going to drive through McDonald's."

"Gavin can't abide Valley food," Betty said teasingly.

"No thanks — we just ate," Geoff answered.

"All right, then, so burgers and fries for me, Mary Kay, Marshall, and..." His eyes lingered on Betty for a moment. Now it was Annie's turn to look away. Betty hesitated, shifting her weight nervously from side to side before letting her eyes fall on Gavin's.

"I'll come with you," Betty said. "I'm trying to eat healthier and need more time to think about what I want."

"Of course," said Gavin. "Are burgers all right with you two?" he asked Mary Kay and Marshall. Marshall nodded and Mary Kay gave the thumbs up, still engrossed in her presentation.

Annie got out her phone and opened Twitter. #ArthurianBreakingNews had taken off, thanks to the efforts of Betty's friends, and it looked like a lot of people would be attending the session. She thought for a moment about telling Mary Kay, but something told her Mary Kay already knew. She put her phone away and leaned back in the armchair and closed her eyes.

At 3:15, Annie, Geoff, Marshall, Betty, Mary Kay, and Gavin arrived in the session room together. Annie imagined them slowly walking through an automatic door in a line that took up the entire hallway with their hair blowing back, like they were a team of superheroes making their entrance together after suiting up. In reality, that's probably not what they looked like at all. They did take up the whole hallway, but in more of a clump, and none of them (except Annie) were really looking ahead of them: Mary Kay and Betty were deep in conversation, both gesticulating wildly, and Gavin was talking to Geoff and Marshall about archaeology while the two grad students held on eagerly to his every word. But the magnitude of their discovery, combined with the enthusiastic response it was already receiving on Twitter (and the fact that when they arrived there were already twenty people in the hallway waiting outside the room) made Annie *feel* like they were a team of superheroes, even if they didn't look like one.

People cleared out of the way when they saw Mary Kay and Betty, and Annie's heart started to flutter with excitement. They entered the room first with Gavin and his giant laptop following close behind. Annie, Marshall, and Geoff filed in with the rest of the people waiting in the hallway and took seats in the second row.

"You guys have your phones ready?" Annie asked, looking at the grad students seated on either side of her.

"For what?" Marshall asked.

"Live-Tweeting."

Geoff pulled out his laptop and turned on the WiFi. "Sending the first Tweet now," he said. "This is getting exciting!"

Session about to begin. Who was King Arthur, really? New evidence, new theories #ArthurianBreakingNews #Kzoo2017

Annie shivered. She was excited too. This was really happening. She held up her phone and took a picture of Mary Kay, looking extremely professional with her blond French twist and dark pink lipstick, and Betty standing beside her with her hands on her hips, looking formidable as always. Annie leaned over to Geoff and whispered, "I think I want to be a combination of the two of them when I grow up."

"I had better watch out then," Geoff replied.

Before Annie could ask him what he meant by that, Geoff turned the other way to talk to whoever was on his left. Annie looked over at Marshall who was staring at his phone. She Tweeted the photo and turned her attention to the front of the room where an older man with a goatee was taking his place at the podium. The session was about to begin.

"Welcome to the third *Early Medieval Europe* session of the weekend," the man said. "Today, we're doing something a little different. Because one of our presenters, Mary Kay McKinley from Seton Hill University, has stumbled upon some, as she is calling it, 'Arthurian Breaking News' along with some other scholars —" he gestured, "— Betty Randall of the University of Michigan, Gavin Chen of Notre Dame University, and Annie Fisher, a graduate student at Michigan, the other presenters have agreed to let Mary Kay begin our session."

Annie sank into her chair. She didn't know that was going to happen. Geoff gave her a high five under the table. Marshall was trying to avoid eye contact, which was fine with Annie. She wasn't sure how she felt about all these people looking at her.

"— if you want to talk about this paper on social media," the man at the podium continued, "please use the hashtag 'Arthurian Breaking News.'"

There was a wave of laughter from some in the audience, but just as many people got out their phones and laptops at the mention of the hashtag. Annie didn't need to look at Twitter herself to know that it was exploding.

"— so without further ado, please give your attention to Mary Kay McKinley, with her collaborative paper, 'Quest for the Historical Arthur: Unexpected findings from History, Poetry, and Archaeology.'"

Everyone applauded as Mary Kay took the podium and pushed the button on her slide show clicker. Annie was surprised to see the first image that came up, alongside the title of the paper, was her own. There in the center of the projector screen were the Lost Sigils of King Arthur surrounded by the Latin inscription, revising the historical memory of King Arthur. Mary Kay clicked the button again and Annie's translation of the Latin appeared at the bottom of the screen.

Annie set aside her phone and devoted her full attention to listening to Mary Kay. Unlike Betty, who gave papers exactly like she talked in normal conversation, Mary Kay put on a sort of presentation voice that was lower and more important-sounding than her natural voice. It seemed to achieve the desired effect — Annie was sure she wasn't the only one in the audience who was captivated by the sound of Mary Kay's voice, even as she made her way through the obligatory introductory material.

"I was originally going to speak to you today about a series of references in sixth- and seventh-century historical writing which all appear to point to the same mysterious figure arising in Britain in the early sixth-century, and suggest that that figure was related to the local warfare in which the Arthur legend originated. That paper would have been a significant step toward not only understanding the historical context of the earliest Arthur tradition, but also demonstrating that people outside Britain — in Gaul, Italy, and even Byzantium — knew about what was going on in Britain at this time. I will still make that argument, and in the first half my talk I will present evidence from Venantius Fortunatus, Jordanes, and a late-sixth-century anonymous historical writer preserved in the extracts of Photius. These sources all seem to describe the same figure, who engaged in disturbing massacres that may have even bordered on genocide.

"Then," she continued, switching the presentation to a slide that showed a photo of Betty's manuscript alongside several photos of the sigils from Gavin's dig, "thanks to the work of my colleagues Betty Randall, who discovered and translated the Welsh poem on the manuscript shown here, and Gavin Chen, who found several inscriptions in west Wales — some of them monumental — that contain these sigils, I will argue that this figure was the historical

King Arthur, and that he made significant headway in his murderous mission before finally being stopped by the real hero, Mordred, who was never remembered for his valiant deeds.

"This is proven by the sigils: magical inscriptions that seem to have been an apotropaic device our Arthur figure employed to protect his territories as he conquered across Britain. According to Gavin Chen, inscriptions like this were part of a complex magical process that has manifested in several ways in early Celtic Britain. Presence of these sigils indicates conquest, and in many cases military occupation. If these sigils belonged to Arthur, then that would suggest that Arthur was the invading party at the Battle of Camlann, rather than a defender.

"This seventh-century poem, which Professor Randall presented on and translated yesterday — you can find her translation on the handout that's making its way around the room right now — presents new evidence for Arthur's final battle and provides context to the sigils and the references in continental authors. As you can see, Mordred was definitely Arthur's adversary at that battle, in which Arthur was particularly ruthless, even through the lens of this pro-Arthur poem. I will take you through the poem again towards the end of the talk, but at the moment I would like to turn your attention to the last line of the introduction, 'Mordred lay forgotten.'

"We would like to suggest that Arthur (and for that matter, Mordred) have been misremembered by history. All the evidence I will present today points to a very different Arthur than the one we know — one who desired to wipe out entire non-Celtic populations from Britain, and one against whom Mordred fought desperately, and, dare I say, heroically. But he was forgotten.

"This brings me to our final piece of evidence." She clicked the clicker again and Annie's photo was back on the screen. "Found sewn into the middle of a sixteenth-century grimoire, these two codex pages, which have yet to be dated definitively but look to be sixth/seventh century based on style and hand, show the very sigils that have been found on monuments throughout Wales surrounded by the Latin inscription, 'Let us scorn the memory of Arthur. Not a hero, but a murderer. Cruel Arthur killed a thousand nations. Mordred could not save them.'"

Mary Kay was silent for a moment, and the whole room went silent with her. Annie turned on her phone screen. Twitter was silent, too. Then, Mary Kay began systematically to go through the evidence. By the end of her talk, there was no one left in the room or on the internet who was not convinced.

| 13 |

Merlin's Book

The discussion after Mary Kay's talk was unbelievable. Gavin and Betty joined her at the front of the room and answered question after question from scholars in all disciplines of medieval studies. People brought up connections that Annie never would have thought of, but once they started talking about them she couldn't believe she hadn't noticed them herself. How could so many generations of people, including scholars who specifically studied Arthurian lore and post-Roman Britain, have gone so long without realizing who Arthur really was?

The conversation on Twitter was just as vibrant. Annie could barely keep up with live-Tweeting the questions and answers, but in the lulls between her own Tweets she noticed more questions and more connections being made online by people who weren't even at the conference. Annie looked over at Marshall's laptop and saw that he was responding to those Tweets, and re-Tweeting some. Lyndsay Solomon and Nora Jean Downey were re-Tweeting everything from the back row. It was only a matter of time before somebody published a Buzzfeed article on this. Then the whole world would know the historical Arthur.

After the excitement of Mary Kay's presentation, the rest of the session was excruciating. No one wanted to be there anymore, but they were all too polite to leave. Annie felt bad for the two other presenters, who knew that no one was there to hear them and that no one seemed to be able to muster even a minimum level of attention after such an exhilarating first paper. Their minds were still on King Arthur, the killer of nations, and Mordred the unsung hero who defeated him once and for all.

Annie kept herself entertained by continuing to follow Twitter, but she longed to get out of the stifling classroom and talk to Mary Kay and Gavin and Betty herself, without the weight of the world on her shoulders. (She made a mental note never to accept a job as a company's social media person.) When the session finally ended, most people filed out of the room, eager to get to the wine hour and keep talking. Only a few people stayed behind. Annie stayed in her seat next to Marshall and Geoff until the room had cleared out fully.

"Whew! That was a whirlwind!" Betty exhaled once they were alone in the classroom. "Does anybody else feel like they need a drink after that?"

"I feel like I need about four drinks, and a cigarette," Mary Kay answered matter-of-factly.

"I'm right there with you," said Gavin. "Shall we hit the bar to celebrate? What is that colonialism place you like, Betty?"

Betty's eyes lit up. "The British Empire?" She turned to the grad students. "What do you guys say? A drink at the British Empire to celebrate our accomplishments?"

"Yeah!" exclaimed Marshall, standing up. "I can't believe we just achieved what we achieved."

"This is really spectacular," said Gavin. "I commend you graduate students on your perseverance and ability to work together with scholars in different disciplines."

"We should all give ourselves a pat on the back for working together across disciplines," said Mary Kay. "It doesn't happen often enough, and it really should. This Kalamazoo conference is the most multidisciplinary conference I attend every year, and every year it splits up into history people over here, material culture people over here, twenty-five different genres of literature people splitting off into twenty-five different cliques. Gower people not talking to Aquinas people, etc."

Betty raised her eyebrows. "Earlier this weekend you didn't even know who Gower was."

"Beside the point. What I'm saying is, we reached these amazing conclusions this weekend because we all worked together."

Annie furrowed her eyebrows. Now that she was no longer caught up in the moment and the room was empty again, the thing that had been bothering her all day, the authenticity of her codex pages, resurfaced. Something wasn't right. There was something missing. It couldn't *possibly* be correct that the reason why generations of scholars never hit upon the truth about King Arthur until now was simply because they had never collaborated across disciplines. The key was her text, and she suddenly had a very bad feeling about it.

"Absolutely right," Marshall was saying. He had packed up his bookbag and was standing at the front of the room with the professors. "I always want to do more collaboration with the History department, but a lot of the time it seems like the English and History departments don't even know each other exists, even though they're right in the same building."

Betty sighed. "I know, it really is a problem, Marshall. Medieval Lunches were meant to bridge the divide between disciplines, but what we always seem to end up with are English people going to

English talks, and Romance Languages people going to Romance Languages talks, and History people going to History talks..."

"I bet you don't even have material culture talks," said Gavin.

"Sometimes we do." It was Annie who spoke. She was remembering the very first Medieval Lunch she had ever attended, when she first met Marshall. She looked at Marshall now and he was smiling at her the exact same way he had smiled at her grimoire the first time he saw it. He was a little too excited. Annie realized that today's event marked a special occasion for Marshall. For some reason that she wasn't privy to, it really mattered to Marshall that the truth about Mordred get out. Now it was out, and he couldn't be happier. Did he know something about the codex he wasn't telling anyone?

"What's wrong, Annie?" Geoff asked just to her. He was the only one who noticed that she was still staring down at her phone, not sharing in the excitement of everyone else.

"Nothing," Annie said. "This Tweet I just saw made me think a little, that's all."

"What did it say?"

She had a fleeting thought that she didn't want to spoil everyone's mood, at least not until after their celebratory drinks, but she brushed it aside. It confirmed her gut feeling, and she knew she had to share. "It's about the codex pages in the grimoire," she said. "We still haven't authenticated it. And I think — not to toot my own horn or anything —" She laughed sheepishly and looked back down at the Twitter app. "But I think the codex in the grimoire is the glue that holds all the other evidence together. If it turns out to be a forgery, the whole theory goes up in flames."

On hearing that, everyone fell silent. They all turned toward Annie, the elation drained from everyone's faces. Marshall just glared. Annie wasn't really used to seeing him without his pervasive smile, but the look he gave her now was more sinister than just a lack of smile.

"What do you mean, 'goes up in flames'?" asked Betty.

Now Annie wished she hadn't said anything. Or waited for a more opportune time to say something. That had always been her problem — timing. She might not have gotten stuck in a bad relationship for all four years of college if she knew how to say what she was thinking at the appropriate time. She shook her head vigorously. That was neither here nor there. Now, in the moment, she had three big deal professors and two fellow grad students staring at her, asking a serious academic question, and she needed to answer it.

"I just think we jumped the gun a little, that's all," she said. Everyone was still staring expectantly, so she continued. "It will be awhile before we can get results from carbon dating, and I know you mentioned that, Mary Kay, so everyone on Twitter knows it, but just the same, we made all these conclusions based on the photographs I took on my phone. None of you even got to see the real thing."

"Don't blame yourself, Annie," Mary Kay started to say.

"I'm not *blaming*," Annie said. She pressed on. "I just think, what we all know, is that we don't know for sure if the codex is authentic or not. Betty researched her manuscript for months and months and months before determining it wasn't a forgery, and only then was she comfortable enough to report it at Kalamazoo. She said it herself — 'You'd all be hearing a very different paper from me today if the manuscript turned out to be false.'"

Betty nodded in agreement.

"But if Betty's had been a forgery, everything would have been fine. We'd still know the same old stuff we've always known about Arthur, which is not much. But if *my* document is a forgery —" She put an emphasis on the "my." Now she really did feel ownership over that mysterious codex hidden in Murray's grimoire. "If *my* document is a forgery, then all the connections we made between

Betty's manuscript and Gavin's inscriptions and the historical references that Mary Kay found kind of fall apart. Think about it: my text mentions Mordred and Arthur, so you know it's about the characters in Betty's poem; then, it includes the sigils, which look like the inscriptions Gavin found. The sigils don't appear anywhere else, though."

"But the sigils were in Jordanes and Fortunatus," Mary Kay interrupted.

"Not exactly," answered Gavin. "We interpreted those mentions of 'signs' to refer to the sigils, but only after we had the sigils in front of us. When you were giving that paper at Shifting Frontiers, though, you didn't think to call me and ask about my trip to Wales, did you?"

Mary Kay shook her head, silent.

"But Mary Kay did make a very convincing argument from the historical texts about the genocidal figure in Britain," Annie continued, "which I think is significant on its own, but that figure could just as well have been Mordred, or someone else. Without the ancient piece of parchment mentioning Mordred and Arthur surrounding the sigils, then, we don't really have anything at all."

"We have something," Betty said reassuringly. "Gavin really did find the sigils that appear on the parchment."

"But we don't know if they're independent," Gavin said. "If Annie's right, and her text is a forgery — which I'll admit has had me worried all along — then some later person could have known about my inscriptions, and Betty's poem, and all the references that Mary Kay found. To me, this whole Arthurian saga is starting to reek of the nineteenth century."

Geoff stifled a laugh. Mary Kay looked up, one corner of her mouth starting to smile while the rest of it fought hard to frown.

"So that's it, then," she said, throwing up her hands. "I was so sure."

Just then, Annie started jamming all her stuff into her bag except for her phone, which she held out in front of her as she made her way to the door.

"Where are you going, Annie?" Geoff asked.

"I'm going to do what I should have done a long time ago," she answered, without looking back. "I'm going to call Murray."

"I have been waiting for you call, Annie," Murray said over the phone in that same calm, even tone he always used. Annie was standing outside of the Schneider building up against a tree with her phone held up to her ear. Geoff, Marshall, Betty, Gavin, and Mary Kay had followed her outside and were standing a few feet away, trying to give her privacy while barely able to contain their interest in what Murray had to say.

"It's about the grimoire," Annie said. "The one you gave me a long time ago. I don't know if you remember —"

"The Spells of Morgan le Fay," Murray replied. "I remember. And I suspect that's the reason you are at Kalamazoo this weekend. You will know our own Betty Randall is presenting this weekend on a new poem about King Arthur, and perhaps you have also heard of a late antique scholar, Mary Kay McKinley —"

"I know — I'm here with them now," Annie said urgently, immediately kicking herself inside for not having spoken to her advisor about this sooner. "I think we made a mistake."

"Oh?" There was interest in Murray's voice.

"I think we may have, um, jumped to some conclusions about the historical King Arthur based on some of the pages in the grimoire that look like they might be ancient. The problem is," — she took a deep breath, embarrassed to admit her failure to yet another person — "I didn't bring the book with me. No one got to see the physical object to check if it's authentic or not. And we gave a presentation —"

Before she could explain the whole situation, Murray interrupted her in the calmest and kindest way possible. "Are you sure you forgot to bring the book?" he asked.

"What?" Annie asked. "Yeah, I didn't bring it. I didn't just forget it. I specifically told my roommate to watch it for me. It's not here."

"I wouldn't be so sure about that," said Murray enigmatically. "Memory is an interesting thing. The human mind has an uncanny knack for fooling itself into remembering the very narrative it wanted to create."

Annie was silent for a moment. Then she asked, "What do you mean?"

"Only what I said. Perhaps if you weren't so focused on the impossibility of dating the codex pages, you might have remembered that you brought the book with you." That was insane, Annie thought. She hadn't even told Murray she was going to Kalamazoo. "But my wife has made dinner — roast beef. I must go. Enjoy the rest of your conference." And then Murray hung up.

Annie stood by the tree for a long time with her phone still held up to her face. Then when she couldn't pretend any longer, she put her phone into her pocket and turned to the rest of the group. "I have to go back to Valley One for a minute," she said.

"What for?" asked Mary Kay.

"I just —" Annie turned and ran all the way back to Valley One, more grateful than ever that she was wearing her jeans and Doc Martens and the orange sweater Gina had found in her closet a lifetime ago.

She could sense the others chasing her back to her room, but she didn't care. She knew Mary Kay couldn't keep up in her heels even if she was a runner, and Betty and Gavin were older, but Marshall and Geoff were right behind her. She skipped the elevator and ran into the stairwell, taking the stairs two at a time until she got to her floor. She could hear the elevator door open and Marshall and

Geoff's voices behind her as she slid her room key into the lock. She didn't have to enter the room to see it right in front of her, staring her in the face. There, on her bed, was the grimoire.

| 14 |

A Most Ancient Magic

Marshall appeared right behind Annie, panting. "Is that the grimoire?" he asked. Suddenly his voice turned angry: "You had it with you *the whole time?*"

"No," Annie said. "Someone must have brought it here." She turned around to face Marshall and Geoff, who were wearing equally surprised faces. "Just give me a minute, okay?" She stepped into the room and closed the door, locking it behind her.

Annie sat down on the bed beside the grimoire and inspected it. She opened it to the middle and saw the two codex pages that she had been looking at in photo form for the past two days. She felt them. They felt different from the other pages. Older. And there was something else, an almost electrifying feeling in her fingers when she touched the page.

This was the same book from her shelf at home, the book that she had entrusted Gina with protecting for the weekend. She had no idea who or what she wanted Gina to protect the book from, but if it was someone who could work magic, which Annie was fully prepared to believe once she saw the book on the bed inside her locked dorm room, there was nothing her roommate could have done. She pulled out her phone and called Gina, who answered on the third ring.

"Hello?" came Gina's voice through the receiver, like nothing was amiss.

"Hey, Gina," Annie started.

"What's up? How's the conference going? Are you going to the dance?"

"Nothing — fine — maybe," Annie blustered. "Hey, do you remember the book I showed you when I was packing to come here?"

"That old medieval book I helped you pack?" Gina asked.

"What?"

"Don't you remember?" Gina asked, laughing a little. "It was this whole big thing. You wanted to make sure it got to the conference super safely. We had to remove two entire pairs of shoes from your suitcase before we put it in, and then I rolled it up in that awful purple blazer of yours to protect it." She paused a minute, and then said more seriously, "You were acting really strange about that book. Really intense."

Annie got up and threw open her suitcase. Sure enough, there was the purple blazer folded up on top of her other clothes. She dug around for a moment and confirmed that the ballet flats she wore the day before were missing, and so were the pumps Gina had packed her for the dance. "Um, Gina?" she asked.

"Yeah?"

"Can you check my closet for a minute and see if my black ballet flats are in there? I thought I packed them, but I must have forgotten them."

Over the phone Annie heard rustling. Then Gina spoke, "Yeah, they're still here. And — hey — so are the heels I lent you! They're right here on your bed. Please tell me you're not going to wear those punk boots to the dance tonight."

Annie smiled at that last comment, but only for a second. Her whole body went cold. Either Gina was playing a massive trick on her — one that involved driving to Kalamazoo and breaking into her dorm room to plant the book and blazer and remove the shoes, and then gaslighting her over the phone — or there was magic at work. The same sort of magic that Annie had definitely felt, but refused to acknowledge, that night over two years ago when she and Marshall read the inscription in the codex.

"I'm probably not going to the dance," Annie said, finally, into the phone.

"Really? Just because you don't have the right shoes? I'm sure it won't be that big of a deal if you wear the boots. I was just giving you shit."

"No — I. I'll have to call you back later. Don't worry about me."

"Why would I be worried about you?"

Annie ignored the question. "I'll be home tomorrow, Gina. See you then." She hoped.

Annie put away her phone and collected herself for a few moments before picking up the grimoire and returning to the door. She opened it to find not just Geoff and Marshall, but Betty, Mary Kay, and Gavin as well all standing in the hallway, waiting for her to emerge.

"You're never going to believe this," Annie said, "but I think Mur— someone sent me the book here. And I think they did it by magic."

Mary Kay busted out laughing, but Betty looked serious. "Let me see that spellbook," she said, pushing her way into the room. The others followed in after her and Annie had no choice but to take a seat on the bed beside Betty and watch her leaf through the grimoire.

When Betty got to the centerfold, she took the parchment between her fingertips and said, "Yes, this definitely feels far older than the rest of the pages." But age was no longer relevant, Annie realized. If this book possessed magical powers, or someone was able to use magic to get it to Annie, then there was no doubt that the pages were authentic. "Morgan le Fay was reputed to be an extremely powerful sorceress," Betty continued. "If this book does contain her spells, then it's possible that it contains some remnants of her magic as well."

"That's what I was afraid of," said Annie. "Betty," she continued, "do you think it's possible that the inscription around the sigils was a spell — a spell to destroy Arthur's memory? And we destroyed Arthur's memory when we read the words?"

Marshall shifted uncomfortably and Gavin started shaking his head. "No, no," Gavin said. "Magic like this is always connected to the material. Showing photos of the page and reading the translation wouldn't have had any effect."

Annie looked up at Marshall, willing him with her eyes to say something. All Marshall did was continue to look around the room — anywhere but at Annie or Gavin. Annie sighed and said, "But I did read the words while holding the parchment. Marshall and I did together, a long time ago. He transcribed the text and I translated it. Then we read it aloud, in English and in Latin."

Gavin and Betty looked at each other, horrified. "That changes everything," said Gavin.

"What does it change?" Marshall interjected. He sounded angry, and Gavin took a step backward into the wall when Marshall moved toward him. "You all made separate discoveries, completely independent of Annie and me. Your discoveries had nothing to do with this book or the spell. Annie and I being here just happened to help you make the connections, but you would have figured it all out anyway."

"I don't know," said Annie softly. "Gavin, when did you find the inscriptions?"

"Last summer," he replied.

"And Betty — the manuscript?"

"Last fall term when I was on sabbatical."

Annie nodded, then turned her gaze to Mary Kay.

"Hmm, well, I've been reading all these texts for a long time," Mary Kay said, "but I don't think I ever noticed the parallels until sometime last year. Maybe two summers ago, I can't remember."

"Doesn't matter," said Annie, a faint smile starting to appear on her lips. "It would have been after Marshall and I cast the spell, two years ago, in the winter."

Mary Kay and Betty nodded, but Marshall turned on Annie, shouting, "What does that have to do with anything? How do you know we were even casting a spell?"

"Because I could feel it!" Annie shouted back, her frustration at Marshall palpable. "Couldn't you? No — don't answer that. I know you could feel it. Don't lie to me, Marshall. You knew it was a spell the entire time, and that's why you were so interested in it in the first place."

Everyone in the room gasped. Gavin turned to Betty and whispered, "This is getting good." Betty whacked him with her purse.

"Okay, so what if I knew it was a spell?" Marshall said defensively.

"Then I want you to reverse it," Annie replied.

"What?" he asked.

"I don't think it's right, what we did to King Arthur. Thanks to the magic of social media, everyone in the world now thinks that Arthur was some sort of genocidal maniac, and every minute that goes by, I feel more and more like that belief is the result of this spell and not the truth."

Mary Kay held up her phone and said, "It's on Buzzfeed now." Everyone ignored her.

Annie held the book out toward Marshall, open to the ancient parchment for him to touch. "Go on," she said. "Read the spell again. Or read it backwards or something."

Marshall hesitated before taking the book from Annie's hands. Gavin stopped him. "That's not how it works," he said. Everyone turned toward him, and he continued, "Or, at least, that's not how most spells of the ancient Romano-British variety worked. You can give it a try. But as far as I know, and I *am* an expert on ancient Celtic and Roman magic, spells were created to do one thing. If we want to reverse that particular spell, we will need to find or create another spell."

"Create?" asked Betty.

"I doubt we have the power to create a spell," Gavin replied. "But this book is full of other spells. I suggest we look there."

"Are you sure about this?" Mary Kay said from the back of the room. She seemed like the only one who wasn't interested in trying to do magic in a Valley One dorm room. Everyone else was huddled around Marshall, who had taken a seat on the bed and started frantically paging through the grimoire, Betty reading over his shoulder with a frown on her face.

"What other choice do we have?" Annie asked Mary Kay.

"Well, we could go back to our respective homes and meet up again next year and try to publish this paper. That's one option I can think of. Another might be just call it a day and not worry about publishing and forget this ever happened."

"I don't think we can forget that easily," Annie replied. "Buzzfeed."

"Right."

"I think we already did some magic, Mary Kay," Annie pleaded. "Now I just want to do a little bit more to try and get us out of this mess we created."

"I'm not sure about that logic. Isn't that what people say about drugs?"

"Shut up, Mary Kay," Betty said from the bed. "The drug metaphor doesn't work here. Annie's right. What we — or more likely she and Marshall two years ago — did was wrong, and we need to fix it. Hopefully there's a spell in here that won't be too complex."

"Okay," Mary Kay replied heavily. "But when the shit hits the fan —" She trailed off, clutching her tote bag.

"I don't think you're going to need that," Marshall replied after a moment. "There's no spell in here that looks like it might reverse the first spell." He did not sound remotely disappointed.

"No," Betty agreed. "But there is this."

"Huh?" Marshall asked, surprised.

Betty had her finger on a page in the middle of the grimoire, right before the page with the sigils. Betty opened to the spell and read the title: "To Confront Thee Adversairie."

"That's so vague," said Marshall. "That will never work. What if we don't all have the same adversary?"

"It's not vague at all," Betty said confidently. "Remember the poem?" She took a folded piece of paper from her pocket — the handout from her and Mary Kay's talks — and read, "*Bedivere led the left flank, brave and strong; He looked toward Arthur for the signal, waiting patiently; To confront the adversary as they trickled around the bend.* There's only one adversary this could refer to, and that is definitively Mordred. Here, Annie." She snatched the book from Marshall's hand and passed it back up to Annie.

"It's probably not going to work, anyway," Marshall said.

Annie shrugged. "There's only one way to find out." She took a deep breath and looked around the room. At Betty's smirk and Gavin's expectant eyes, Mary Kay's nervous smile and Geoff's warm one. And Marshall. She didn't know what to make of Marshall. "Here goes," she said. Running her finger along the single line of Latin text, she spoke aloud the magic words.

The exact moment she finished uttering the spell, a light appeared on the other side of the door that led to the hallway and the door itself started to shake. Everyone stood still for a moment, too shocked that something even happened to go near the door. Finally, it was Geoff who bravely stepped forward. He put an arm out to shield everyone else and slowly pulled open the door. Past the threshold was not the shabby dorm hallway, but rather a foggy meadow in the evening, sounds, smells and all.

Betty spoke first. "A portal? You have got to be fucking kidding me."

Annie stashed the grimoire in her bag and stood beside Geoff. "Our adversary must be out there. Who's coming?"

"If you're going I'm coming with you," Geoff whispered, grasping Annie's hand. Annie gave Geoff's hand a squeeze and put one foot outside the door.

"Come on, Mary Kay," Betty said softly.

"Sure," Mary Kay whispered. "Just let me put on some lipstick first."

"Marshall and I are right behind you," announced Gavin, steering the younger man toward the door.

Then, once again with the air of a team of superheroes on their way to a final battle, the six medievalists stepped out into the fog.

| 15 |

The Adversary

Wales, 537

Mordred could sense something was amiss. He went outside onto the battlement, even though he knew he wouldn't be able to see anything in such dense fog. He was right. Visibility was less than a mile. All about him was fog. But as he looked toward the west, he got the unmistakable feeling that something, or someone, was coming. He needed to prepare. He hurried inside the fortress to ready his troops.

No sooner did he arrive in the great hall than a messenger came banging on the door, crying to be let in. A servant opened the door and the messenger flew straight to Mordred, collapsing at his feet.

"What is it you want?" Mordred spat.

"It is the Lady Morgan," the messenger gasped.

Mordred's blood went cold. How could she know? How could she have found out that Merlin saw the codex, that Merlin had supplied the parchment? The sense of foreboding he felt out on the battlement — could that be Morgan? Or something more sinister that

Morgan was coming to warn him about? The messenger, catching his breath, answered his unspoken question.

"The Lady Morgan knows you worked with Merlin," he said. "And that will be your downfall. She is on her way now to help protect you against whatever forces Merlin is sending. They are on their way."

Mordred helped the messenger to his feet. "Go in the kitchens. Have something to eat." Then he yelled for the servant. "Boy! See to it that this messenger's horse is fed and watered."

"No need, sir," the messenger said, shaking his head. "My horse died about a mile back. Morgan will be furious at me for getting to you so late. Thank you for your hospitality. I will go to the kitchens now. But you must barricade this entire fortress behind all its defenses and wait here for Morgan. She will be able to help you."

"But how will Morgan get in?"

The messenger turned back to Mordred and smiled, a knowing smile made more unsettling by the fact that the messenger utterly lacked teeth. "She will find a way."

Morgan arrived several hours later while Mordred huddled against a cold, stone wall inside the crumbling Roman fortress. He was starting to question his actions. Perhaps Morgan was being paranoid. Maybe no one was coming after all. Or perhaps no one was coming and Morgan had played a malicious trick on him. Then all of a sudden, Morgan appeared, entering quietly through the doorway to the fortress's cellar where Mordred hid. She looked more radiant than she had the last time they met, a residual effect of the magic she had used to penetrate Mordred's fortress.

"You showed Merlin the parchment," she said, staring accusingly into Mordred's eyes, willing him to admit his mistake.

"I did, I did, milady. I am so sorry."

"You showed him the parchment after I told you not to."

Mordred felt as if every muscle inside his body was being manipulated by an outside force. Rather than lie like he wanted to, he shook his head from side to side. Then he felt his mouth form the words, and his lungs supply the air, as he was forced to say, "No, milady. Merlin already knew about the parchment and the spell I was trying to forge. I lied to you."

"Thank you," replied Morgan, taking a seat on one of the boxes on the opposite end of the wall. "You will be truthful with me now." It was a command, and Mordred had the strange feeling that it was also a spell. "But I will have you know, I do not like it when people waste my magic. Do you have any idea what it cost me to forge that spell of yours? And now, to see its power threatened because Merlin had his dirty hands in it makes me very unhappy indeed. That is why I am offering to help you."

"Thank you, thank you, milady," Mordred breathed. "I will never be able to repay my gratitude in full."

"I'm not doing it for you," Morgan snapped. She pushed back her long dark hair in a single fluid motion and Mordred was brought to his knees. "I'm doing it to save my spell. You see, Merlin's magic is not quite like mine. It is subtler. Merlin had not the power to destroy my spell — or if he did, he would not use it in precisely that way. Rather, what Merlin did was attach the spell to himself, to ensure that whoever used it would always be called back to him, and he could always help them."

They were silent for a moment before Mordred asked, "So what does that mean? What happened to the spell?"

"The spell worked," Morgan said, examining her long fingernails in the light of the dim fire. "But now Merlin has sent some avengers to destroy you. If you die now, in this time, before a future holder of the parchment has a chance to speak the words you created, the spell will come to naught."

"So that means," Mordred said slowly, "we will have to do battle?"

"Not just do battle," said Morgan with a smile, "but you must utterly destroy all those who Merlin sent for you without being killed yourself. That is why I am offering to help you. You have no chance against them on your own. You and your ruined fortress and your tiny army. They would destroy you in a heartbeat. But with me, and of course my magic, by your side, I would say your odds look pretty good."

Mordred got up from the floor and brushed the dirt off his knees. He paced for a moment, trying not to look at Morgan and her seductive smile.

"Don't worry, my pet," Morgan said. "Everything will be all right with Auntie Morgan here by your side."

Mordred turned violently and stared back at the witch. How dare she patronize him. "We prepare for battle now," he said in a low voice. "No more of this hiding like rabbits. We make ready, and we fight. Whatever is coming after us, we will be prepared. I will be victorious, and all will remember me as a hero."

Morgan grinned, showing all her dazzling teeth. "That's right, dear," she said, standing up from her perch. It was only then that Mordred realized that provoking his anger had also been part of Morgan's plan.

| 16 |

The Fort

Annie held tight to Geoff's hand as she walked through the fog looking straight ahead. She had no idea where she was going, only that she could not turn back. For a time, the only sounds were six pairs of footsteps crunching through the frosted grass and the wind whistling far away. Annie shivered and Geoff put his arm around her. They kept walking.

Gavin finally spoke, breaking the eerily tranquil calm with his analytical voice. "I know where we are," he said. Annie turned around and saw that everyone else was shivering too. Betty pulled her paisley scarf tight around her body. Mary Kay was holding a crimson and gold umbrella to shield herself against the blowing mist. Far off in the distance, Annie could no longer see the door to her dorm room. She wondered if it was still there in the middle of the meadow or if it had disappeared entirely.

"We are in Wales," Gavin said, "not far from where the Battle of Camlann is thought to have taken place. There are a few Roman ruins around here. I think we should look for one and take shelter in there, at least until we can get our bearings."

"Our bearings for what?" Mary Kay asked. Her teeth were chattering.

Gavin didn't answer. He strode ahead of Annie and started steering their group a little to the right. Everyone followed him without speaking. After a few moments, Annie could see a structure appear on the horizon. "Are there any sigils around here, Gavin?" she asked.

"Yes, as a matter of fact, there are, if we are where I think we are."

"And what would that mean?" asked Betty.

"It would depend on whether we're in Wales *now*, or if we have also traveled in time as well as space. Ever since I figured out where we were I've believed we are in the Wales of King Arthur." He gazed up ahead at the fortress. "If it is the sixth century, that fortress isn't likely to be empty. It's either held by Arthur and his men, or..." No one needed him to finish his sentence, though. If the fortress was not held by Arthur's men, then they were about to confront their adversary much sooner — and with much less preparation — than they had anticipated.

"So should we start looking around for an inscription, to see if Arthur marked out this base as his?" asked Mary Kay.

Gavin shrugged. "You can if you want. If enemies hold the fortress, though, they'll see us coming before we can get close enough to spot a sigil."

"Then what do we do?" asked Betty, panicked.

"We just keep walking."

Annie took a deep breath and pulled Geoff's arm more tightly around herself. Without a word, she and Geoff fell into step behind Gavin and walked another twenty minutes, watching the structure in the distance grow larger and larger until she was sure that if the adversary did hold the fort, they'd be shooting arrows at them by now.

Finally, they were close enough to see light coming from one of the windows. A fire. This was fortunate, as dark was descending quickly.

"Is that fire good or bad?" Betty whispered. She was now walking right behind Gavin and leaned into him to ask the question.

"Judging by the fact that it's not being hurled out that window at us, I'd say good," said Gavin.

"And it's probably warmer than it is out here," said Mary Kay.

"Don't get your hopes up," Gavin quipped.

The party trudged the remaining two hundred yards to the walls of the fortress and were practically frozen by the time they reached it. It was farther away than it looked. When they got to the gate unscathed, they felt confident that whoever was inside did not mean to harm them, at least not immediately.

"All right, I guess we make our presence known somehow," said Gavin.

Everyone stared at him, shivering, waiting for him to bang on the gate or call up to the tower or do whatever it was he intended to do to make their presence known. When Gavin didn't move, but actually took a step backward now that he realized the risk he was about to take, Geoff moved forward instead.

"Come on, guys," he said. "It's going to be okay." Still holding fast to Annie's hand with his left hand, he cupped his right hand around his mouth and called out, "Halloooooo!"

When no one responded, Marshall pushed his way to the front of the group and began heaving his body against the wooden door with all his might.

"What are you doing, Marshall?" Annie asked. She had almost forgotten he was with them — he had been silent for their entire walk.

"I need to find out who's in this castle," he said, his teeth clenched tight together.

"Hold on, Marshall," Betty said. "That's what we're all trying to do. Just wait for someone to answer."

"No." Marshall turned around abruptly. "I'm not with you. I'm sorry, Betty. I'm not on your side." Then he turned to Annie and stared at her so meanly he didn't look like Marshall anymore. Annie gasped in shock, and Marshall started to laugh. "Are you really so surprised, Annie? I thought you had figured it out a long time ago. I thought that's why you stopped talking to me after we cast the spell — because you knew I *wanted* to destroy Arthur's memory. No matter. You all know now."

Marshall turned around, but before anyone could say or do anything, the door opened wide and a solitary, unarmed guard met the group. "Greetings in the name of King Arthur!" the man announced. Everyone but Marshall breathed a sigh of relief.

Then Marshall pushed his way past the door guard and took off into the fortress. While the guard was still getting back on his feet, Marshall galloped past on a stolen horse, almost trampling all his friends on his way through the gate. "Long live Mordred!" he called behind him as he rode off into the night.

"Hurry," the door guard said to the group, waving them in. "We think Mordred is encamped a day's ride away. If that man truly means to betray you to the enemy, we haven't much time to prepare for battle."

Annie gave Geoff's hand another squeeze and followed the guard inside the fort.

They group minus Marshall followed the guard through a vibrant but run-down Roman fort. They passed a stable just inside the gate and Annie wondered whether Marshall knew it would be that easy to steal a horse once the gate had opened. It was unguarded, as it was night and most of the inhabitants of the town were probably asleep in the handful of small huts that were scatted throughout the settlement. They turned beside an old stone well and passed the crumbling stone chapel before entering a large stone building at the back of the fort.

It took a moment for Annie's eyes to adjust to the darkness inside the long, rectangular hall that made up the ground floor of the building. There were no windows, and the only light seemed to be coming from a few candles mounted in hanging light fixtures at the far end of the room. The first thing Annie noticed was that light fixtures actually extended the length of the room — there was one right above her head — but only a few contained candles. The second thing she noticed was that under the lit candles sat a single piece of furniture. It was a large, heavy-looking wooden table, and it was round. She gasped.

"Is that the —" she started to ask.

"Welcome to the great hall," announced the guard who was leading them. "This is where King Arthur and his knights have been meeting, and this is where we knights will meet with you presently. I am Bedivere. I am pleased to make your acquaintance."

"*You're* Sir Bedivere?" Betty asked, a little too loudly. Then she cleared her throat and dipped into an awkward curtsy. "I mean, it is an honor to meet you, Sir Bedivere. I've read so much about you — you are a figure of legend."

Mary Kay stifled a snort.

"Please excuse my colleague," Betty continued. "I am Betty Randall, and my companions are Mary Kay McKinley, Gavin Chen, Annie Fisher, and Geoff Porter."

Bedivere took off his hat and bowed slightly. "It is an honor to meet all of you. Your coming has been foretold."

"What do you mean, foretold?" Betty asked.

"The great wizard Merlin warned us after Arthur's final battle that someone may come from the future to avenge his memory."

"Arthur's dead?" asked Gavin.

Bedivere shook his head. "I have not received word yet. He was injured in battle against Mordred and we all fear that the wound is mortal. He has gone to Avalon to spend his last days."

There was silence for a moment. Then Bedivere continued, "Merlin arrived here yesterday to warn us. He did not say whom he would send, but he did say that it would be someone who did not look anything like us." Bedivere glanced around at Annie's boots and Mary Kay's pantsuit and Annie nodded.

"That would be us," Annie said. "We accidentally did a spell that changed the way people remembered Arthur. He was a good man, wasn't he?"

Bedivere closed his eyes in reverence. "The best. Never in my life have I met a kinder or more just soul."

"What can we do, then?" Annie asked. "What can we do to reverse the spell? What did Merlin tell you these avengers were supposed to do?"

Bedivere opened his eyes and stared grimly around at the group. "You must defeat Mordred. He is still alive, waiting for someone to read the spell. In our time, the spell has not been cast yet. That means it is not too late. If you can defeat him before the spell can come into the hands of someone who has never known Arthur, then it will be broken."

"You do mean in battle, don't you?" asked Gavin. Everyone turned to look at him.

"How else do you propose to defeat Mordred?" Bedivere asked calmly. "He must be killed. Unless one of you is able to poison him, or to strangle him in his sleep, then battle will be the way he shall fall." He took a deep breath and glanced over his shoulder. "Judging by the speed at which your companion was moving on his horse just now, I would not be surprised if his army arrives to do battle tomorrow."

"Great, well, we're all dead," said Mary Kay.

Bedivere raised an eyebrow. "We have made preparations for battle. You need only to eat and to rest and be ready for the morrow. I have sent for the other knights to be awakened and a meal to be prepared for you. The knights should be arriving shortly. You may take your seats in the meantime." He gestured to the table behind him and Annie felt a jolt of excitement — was she going to have a meal at the actual Round Table?

Bedivere made to go through a door behind the round table but stopped first and turned around. "I believe I now understand what Merlin's prophecy meant," he said. "You did not arrive with a plan to destroy Mordred, but your arrival was the impetus for his attack."

"What do you mean?" Betty asked.

"The member of your party who stole one of our horses," Bedivere stated as if it were obvious. "*He* will incite Mordred to come attack *us*. Mordred will come — I know it. But we will be fighting him on the defensive. I suggest you eat well tonight and go right to sleep. Tomorrow is going to decide not only the fate of ourselves, but also of Arthur, the greatest king of the Britons."

| 17 |

A Medieval Feast

Bedivere was barely gone two minutes before several women entered the room from a large wooden door that led outside. They brought candles, which they screwed into the hanging fixtures and their dim, smoky light revealed colorful tapestries hanging on the walls. Annie gasped in awe and started choking on the smoke from the burning tallow. Here she was, in post-Roman Britain, a place she was vaguely familiar with from reading, but could not have imagined would be as beautiful and as sad as it actually was.

Betty was glancing around too, focusing especially on the women, dressed in layers of brown fabric, who were now setting the table with bowls and goblets made from a combination of carved wood, poorly-thrown ceramic, and ornate silver. "So this is Arthur's England, huh?" Betty asked after a minute.

"What were you expecting?" Mary Kay replied, "Camelot?"

"Yeah," teased Gavin. "Rows of horses clad in brightly-colored garments, men walking around wearing shining armor and swinging broadswords? Maids in laced-up corsets and conical head-dresses?"

"Tons and tons of light from wax candles?" added Mary Kay, grinning.

"Perhaps a minstrel with a lute?" said Geoff.

Betty was laughing. "Stop it, you guys. I'm not a historian."

"We know," said Mary Kay.

"But, to answer your question," Gavin said, no longer teasing, "this is Arthur's England. It is still remarkably Roman. And yet, it is completely different in the ways this culture used and reused the material left over from its past."

"Like American cities today," Geoff whispered. He was grinning.

"If I weren't scared to death I'd never make it home, I'd be having the time of my life right now," breathed Mary Kay, fingering a silk covering on the sideboard where servants were now placing pots and trays full of food.

"Don't think of it like that, Mary Kay," Betty said. "Enjoy yourself now."

"But what if I never get to tell anyone what I saw here?"

"Stop it! I don't believe that is true, but even if it were, it's out of our control. Just try to go along for now, and trust that Arthur's army is sufficient to defeat Mordred."

Mary Kay clutched her tote bag and opened her mouth like she was going to say something else, but shut it. The door behind the Round Table opened again and Bedivere was back. With him were two other men who were surely other knights of the round table, and a woman whose beauty transcended the ages. She had long brown hair that was twisted back into a braid that was just visible under a light blue veil and wore a simple dress of darkest blue. Her skin seemed to glow in the golden candlelight and her blue eyes shone like crystal. She looked at Annie and her small, pink lips parted into something of a smile. "Guinevere," Annie whispered.

"Ladies and gentlemen," Bedivere announced, "I would like you to meet some of my fellow knights. This is Kei," he said, gesturing to the bigger and blonder of his two companions, "and Gawain. The queen, Guinevere, will sit in Arthur's seat."

Everyone seemed to hold their breath as Guinevere walked around the table and took her place in the seat nearest Geoff. "You may now be seated," she said in a voice that sounded like it came from another world.

Geoff moved first, and sat in the seat beside Guinevere. Annie sat beside Geoff. On her left sat Betty, and Mary Kay next to her. Bedivere, Kei, Gavin, and Gawain sat on the other side of Queen Guinevere. Then Bedivere spoke: "Knights and lady, I present to you the foretold avengers: Gavin Chen, Mary Kay McKinley, Geoff Porter, Betty Randall, and Annie Fisher. It will be up to us to share with them our strategy, but first, they need to be nourished. They have traveled a long way."

The door to the outside opened again and the servant women returned carrying a large tray on which some humongous dead bird rested — the entree. They set the bird in the middle of the table and began uncovering the various pots and plates they had already brought in, revealing a variety of root vegetables and stews. One of them lifted a flagon of wine from the table and began filling their cups. Another started cutting pieces off of the bird and distributing them onto everyone's plates.

The knights immediately started digging in. "Boy, you must be special if they're roasting the pheasant for you!" Kei exclaimed, tearing off a huge bite of the bird's leg with his teeth and chewing loudly. Mary Kay recoiled at the sight, looking even less interested in this medieval meal than she had been in her breakfast the morning before.

As if reading her mind, Betty said, "I'm sure it's all right. They're eating it, aren't they?"

"Their digestive systems are used to their food," Mary Kay replied.

"Don't think about it," said Geoff. He picked up a vegetable and put it in his mouth. "It doesn't taste bad at all. Interesting flavor, actually."

"You can't always taste the bacteria that are about to ravage your stomach," Mary Kay said through clenched teeth.

"He's right though," said Gavin. "We're stuck here now, at least until we defeat Mordred —"

"We think."

"We think. But we'll have more energy to fight tomorrow if we eat our supper tonight."

"Alternatively," argued Mary Kay, "we'll have more energy tomorrow if we skip dinner tonight than if we spend all night puking our guts out."

"Enough!" cried Betty. She picked up a piece of pheasant meat and took a bite. "I trust this meat. You know why? Because it's *magic*. We just *time traveled*, for fuck's sake. These guys *speak our language*. Or we speak theirs. And you're worried about the food? Come on."

Mary Kay reluctantly took a piece of the pheasant and some dense, granular bread, but refused to touch the vegetables. That was a shame, thought Annie. The stews were surprisingly delicious. She would have to remember to cook more with beets and turnips once she got back to the present. She refused to let herself think about the possibility that she might not be able to get back to the present.

For a few moments after that, everyone ate in silence, not realizing how hungry they were. Then, when Bedivere had finished eating he stood at his seat and spoke to the group: "Most of you know why we are here this evening," he said. The other knights and Guinevere nodded, and Annie followed along and nodded too. "The moment is at hand. The moment Merlin warned us about three days ago. Soon, and I believe it may be as soon as tomorrow, the armies of Mordred will come to attack us. There is more at stake than just our lives. These visitors have been sent to destroy Mordred. If they succeed, then Arthur will be remembered as the hero he truly is. If they fail, however, I fear that our king will go down in history and legend as a murderer of entire nations."

Guinevere gave a small gasp and looked down at her lap. Geoff instinctively turned to comfort her.

Bedivere continued, "Now is the time to strategize. We gather here at the Round Table for the very purpose for which Arthur had it created. To plan for war." He cleared his throat. "Gawain, Kei, and I have all been making ready our armies."

The other two knights nodded through bites of pheasant.

"We mean to do better than we did at Camlann," Bedivere continued. "And the wing of the army that Arthur commanded is now without a leader. We will need one of you to take command of that army." As he spoke, Bedivere's eyes fell on Geoff. Geoff nodded stoically, and Annie gasped.

"You can't command an army, Geoff!" she said automatically.

Bedivere chuckled. "Sure he can," he said. "Do not worry about Geoff. It is a well-trained army, and he will be receiving commands from us."

"But —" Annie started to protest, but Bedivere cut her off.

"Furthermore, since we will be the ones under attack, we will need someone to defend the fortress." He turned to Gavin. "You looked comfortable moving around the fort today — no doubt you are familiar with the layout."

Gavin nodded, saying nothing.

"Good. It is settled." Then he turned to Betty, Mary Kay, and Annie. "It is not proper for women to engage in physical combat, but the three of you will be able to attack and defend with magic. We can be sure the opposing side will use magic too, if Mordred is still conspiring with that witch Morgan, as our intelligence reports tell us he is. We will need to counter with magic of our own."

"What magic?" asked Annie. "We don't know any magic."

Bedivere looked taken aback. "You got here, did you not?"

Annie nodded. The book. Would the spells in that grimoire be enough to defeat Morgan le Fay? If the spells it contained actually did belong to her, wouldn't she know them already and be able to anticipate them?

Bedivere smiled again and clapped his hands. "Wonderful. Now, Kei, Gawain, please brief us on your armies. I want everyone to be familiar with everyone's plans so there will be no surprises tomorrow."

The meeting went on for almost an hour, and Annie was sleepy by the end of it. After the feast, which culminated in a strange, gelatinous dessert that was supposed to be their reward for sitting through lengthy reports on infantrymen, horses, melee weapons, and range weapons, Bedivere announced that they should go straight to bed — they would have to be battle-ready before dawn. He then grabbed Geoff and Gavin by the arms and steered them out the back door before they could say good night. Kei and Gawain followed them, and the women were left alone in the hall with Guinevere.

Guinevere had hardly spoken the entire meal. Once the men were out of the room, she spoke comfortably in a friendly tone that made Annie feel like she was being taken care of.

"Don't worry too much about tomorrow," she said. "Bedivere is very serious and sometimes makes things sound a lot worse than they are. Much is at stake, but you should not feel the pressure he does. You've already come so far! You came here, didn't you? That means you're halfway to breaking the spell." Annie hadn't thought of it like that before, but Guinevere had a point. "You may think the battle tomorrow will be the hardest part of your trial, but it is not. You already figured out you needed to defeat Mordred, and you already took the steps necessary to finding him. You took the biggest leap of faith of all — into the past. I commend your bravery."

"Thank you," Annie said, unable to suppress a smile.

"Yeah," said Mary Kay, "when you put it that way, I guess we did do something. Do you really think we're halfway to defeating Mordred, though?"

Guinevere smiled radiantly, showing all her teeth: "I know so. Bedivere is right about one thing, though. We all need our rest. We especially will need energy for our magic."

"But what kind of magic will we do?" asked Betty.

"I am gifted in healing," said Guinevere, "so I will be on hand to tend to the wounded. You three will want to use magic to defend the fort, do battle with Morgan, and most importantly, seek out Mordred and destroy him. It is possible that he will be destroyed by the sword of one of our men, but it is equally possible that he will be hit by a curse. With magic, we have the power of anticipation, far more so than in hand-to-hand combat. Whatever spells you prepare tomorrow, make sure there is at least one designed to take down Mordred. Come, I will show you to your bed chamber."

Guinevere led Annie, Betty, and Mary Kay outside into the cold night and into a stone tower at the back corner of the fortress. Inside, they ascended a set of narrow stairs and emerged in a low-ceilinged room where a fire burned between two straw mattresses covered with blankets. The only other piece of furniture in the room was a wood box, from which Guinevere pulled three wool robes and passed them around. "You will sleep here tonight," she said. "You may leave the fire burning. I will return in the morning to wake you."

"Thank you for your hospitality, Queen Guinevere," Betty said, bowing slightly.

Guinevere's lips parted in acknowledgment. "It's just Guinevere now," she said, before disappearing into the stairwell, closing the door behind her.

"Whew!" Betty announced when Guinevere had left. "I'm exhausted. Let's get to bed. MK — you bunking with me? We'll let Annie have her own bed."

"Actually," said Mary Kay, "it's freezing in here. Annie might prefer to sleep with us, just like people would have done back then. And we can use all the blankets. What do you think, Annie?"

Annie considered the offer. The first thought that came to her mind was that she was about to share a bed with two huge big deal professors — it couldn't get much more intimate than that. Then she started to laugh. She had to get over this ridiculous celebrity shock — she had traveled to the past with these people. If they weren't her friends now, then Annie probably didn't belong at the conference after all. "All right," she said. "I don't move around in my sleep much, and I think you're right, it will be warmer."

"Perfect," said Betty. She was already removing her clothes and putting on the itchy wool nightgown that Guinevere had given her. "Now let's all turn in. We have a busy day ahead of us tomorrow."

"Yeah," Mary Kay sighed, sitting on the end of the straw mattress. She still hadn't unfolded her nightgown. "I just don't know. This whole situation really freaks me out, you know? How did we get here? What if we *can't* destroy Mordred? We should have planned a little back at Kalamazoo before reciting the spell. Brought back drones or something, a little twenty-first century advantage."

Betty sat down beside Mary Kay and put her arm around her. "We're not going to need drones," she said. "We have something better. We have Merlin."

"What do you mean?"

QUEST FOR THE HISTORICAL ARTHUR - 137

"Merlin's spell brought us here, and Merlin is the most powerful wizard there ever was. Seriously — if he could bring us through time and space through a portal that opened up in a dorm at Kalamazoo, do you really think he's going to leave us to fend for ourselves in a medieval battle, totally?"

Mary Kay smiled. "Well, when you put it that way." She looked down into her hands again and Betty started rubbing her back.

"It'll be okay, Mary," she said. "If Merlin can bring us back to this moment, he can also bring us home. And he will."

Mary Kay's stomach rumbled.

"And he can also make sure we can digest the food — that I'm positive of. You should really eat tomorrow."

Mary Kay smiled weakly and sighed. "I have some granola bars in my bag. I'll eat one now. You guys can have one if you want."

"Thanks, but I'm beat. Good night."

Annie put on her nightgown and crawled into bed beside Betty, who slept in the middle. "Good night," she said, before turning on her side to face the fire.

Annie lay awake for a long time that night — long after Betty's and Mary Kay's breathing both slowed down. She was thinking about the two of them, actually, about their confusing relationship. When she first met them at Kalamazoo, ages and ages — two days — ago, she thought they hated each other or resented each other or something. Now she realized that it was much more complicated than that. They were completely different people, but somehow they complemented one another. They seemed to know each other really well, and really care for each other. That, in Annie's mind, made them friends.

Annie wished she had a friend like that. She never really made any close girl friends in college — her intense, long-term relationship with Chad had seen to that. Her historian friends at Michigan were more like coworkers, fun to hang out with, but not really close. Her closest friend was her roommate Gina, and she knew Gina cared about her and she could probably talk to Gina about anything if she asked, but they weren't really *close* close.

Then she thought about Marshall. Marshall had seemed like he could be a good friend when she first met him. He was non-threatening, at least, and they shared an interest in Arthuriana. But then when Annie realized that he was only using her for her grimoire, she let him go. She wasn't sure why she was so eager to hang out with him at Kalamazoo. She thought, perhaps, it was because he was familiar. Someone else from Michigan whom she already knew, and someone who had a connection to Betty, whom she wanted meet. Marshall was never really her friend. So if that was the case, then why did she feel so betrayed when Marshall abandoned their party for Mordred earlier that evening?

She pondered that last question for a long time, until eventually fatigue overtook her and she drifted off to sleep.

| 18 |

Dawn of Battle

It was still dark when Annie awoke suddenly. The fire had burned down to the embers and Betty and Mary Kay were still fast asleep. Annie was trying to figure out what woke her when she noticed two shadowy figures moving in the corner. "Guinevere, is that you?" she whispered.

"Oh good, you're awake," replied Guinevere. "I was just coming to rouse you. The armies are already outside preparing for battle. I brought you some clothing to wear. You may keep your personal belongings in the chest here — they will be safe." Guinevere's servant handed Annie a pile of clothing and set the rest of the clothes she was carrying on the empty mattress.

"Thank you," Annie replied. She started to climb out of the blankets but quickly crawled back in once she felt the frigid air on her skin.

"Aelwen, please build up this fire for the visitors so they have heat while they dress," Guinevere said to the other woman. "They are not used to our ways. Annie, can you wake your companions and be down in the hall within the quarter hour? You can have something to eat, and then we will prepare our spells."

Guinevere was gone as soon as Annie could nod in assent.

Mary Kay and Betty woke up a moment later at the sound of Aelwen stoking the fire. "Is it morning already?" Mary Kay asked, rubbing her eyes. "Agh, I slept in my contacts! That was a bad idea."

"It's morning" Annie said. "Guinevere has already been in. Aelwen brought us clothes and more wood for the fire. Once it gets a little warmer in here we need to get dressed and then meet downstairs for breakfast. Guinevere wants to get started with the magic right away."

"All finished," Aelwen said.

"Thank you," said Annie. Aelwen bowed and left the room as quickly and silently as Guinevere had.

"Right, the magic," Betty said, rubbing her eyes.

"I know," Annie replied. She glanced at her tote bag, which was in a pile with Betty's purse and Mary Kay's bag on the other side of the room. "I guess we should take a look at the grimoire."

"I can help you read it," Betty offered, "while I wait to warm up." She shivered and burrowed back under the covers. Annie got up and brought her conference bag over to Betty who started leafing through the grimoire while Annie got dressed.

The clothes she had been given were not much different from the shift-like night dress she was already wearing. There was a pair of tannish wool tights with a string she assumed she was supposed to use to hold them up at her waist, some sort of dress made of a heavier material than her night dress that also came with a rope to tie it around her waist, and a greenish stole that went over the dress. There was also a drab floppy hat that she decided to save for last. She started to take off her night gown, but Mary Kay stopped her.

"No," she said. "You can put that on over your night dress. That way you will be warmer."

"Good thinking," said Annie, who picked up the tights and pulled them on under her night dress. She immediately felt warmer.

When she finished getting dressed, two odd pieces of leather she hadn't noticed before were left on the ground. "What are these?" Annie asked, picking one up.

"Those would be shoes," replied Mary Kay, who was now getting dressed herself. "And thank God there are shoes, because whatever today has in store for me, I don't think I can do it in those heels." She picked up her black pumps and put them in the wooden chest on top of her neatly folded pant suit and flowered blouse.

Annie examined the shoe more closely and frowned. "I think my boots will be more comfortable," she concluded.

"Then by all means, wear the boots," said Mary Kay. "No need to suffer for the sake of historical accuracy. I'm not taking my contacts out."

"In that case, I think I'll wear my own shoes too," said Betty, who was now more than halfway through the grimoire.

When they had all gotten dressed and were warming themselves by the fire, Annie asked, "Are we ready to go down?" She decided not to ask Betty if she found any useful spells in the grimoire. The frown on the older woman's face told her she did not.

Betty answered with another question: "Do you think we'll get a chance to wash our faces or something first? I feel so grimy."

"Do you really want to put freezing water on your face today?" Mary Kay asked. "I can see your breath."

"Come on," said Annie, now impatient. "Let's go down."

The knights were already in the hall with Guinevere when Annie and the others entered. "Oh good, you're here!" exclaimed Guinevere. "I was just about to come up and fetch you. The knights are all ready to depart. They would have been off by now, but these two insisted they meet with you first."

Two men dressed in padded leather armor and headgear and holding humongous bronze shields stepped forward, and it took a moment before Annie recognized them as Geoff and Gavin. Geoff came up to Annie and took her hand and kissed it. "Sorry," he said as soon as he did it. "I think it's the clothes. I'm dressed like a Knight of the Round Table and you look stunning in that noble lady outfit."

"Thank you," Annie said, grinning. "This is a noble lady outfit?"

"I think so, but he would know for sure." Geoff gestured with his shield at Gavin, who was down on one knee performing a similar feat of chivalry in front of Betty. "Anyway, I'm about to go into battle." He laughed. "I can't believe I'm saying that out loud. My younger brother joined the navy last year and I couldn't believe he was going to fight in battles halfway across the world. I thought it was selfish. Like he didn't care about our mom or family at all. Now — well I still can't really say that I *get* it. But I don't blame him, you know?"

Annie nodded. She really didn't know what to say. She was finally registering the fact that Geoff was about to go into battle. He was literally about to carry a sword and a shield and charge at other people carrying swords and shields and charging at him. At least he got a horse. She choked back a sob and threw her arms around Geoff. "You don't have to go, you know," she whispered into his ear.

"Annie, I have to," Geoff whispered soothingly.

"You don't. You can stay back with us. We're supposed to work the magic. It's still fighting. It's just like the guys driving the drones rather than the people on the front lines. Come on and do it with us."

Geoff tried to laugh, but it came out like a sob too. "I have to go, Annie. King Arthur's away in Avalon, dying. They need someone to command his wing. I feel like I need to do this."

Annie took a step back and wiped away tears from her eyes. "If you're sure," she managed to whisper.

A few feet away, Gavin was having a completely different con-versation with the other women. "Take me with you," he pleaded, still on his knees.

"Get up, Gavin," said Betty, pursing her lips. "This doesn't look good."

"You don't understand," said Gavin. "I'm old! I can't go into battle! But I am good at strategy. Can't I stay back with you and work magic? That would be contributing, wouldn't it? Like Annie said — driving the drones?"

Betty put her arm on Gavin's, trying to comfort him. "But Gavin, they need you on the ground. You know the lay of the land. You know the future locations of stuff that doesn't exist yet! Can't you see how valuable that will be in battle?"

Gavin nodded. "I see how that makes sense, logically. But I really don't think I belong on the battlefield at my age. I would be dead by now if I were living in their time period anyway!"

"Yeah," said Mary Kay, "because you would have already *died in battle*. Now pull up your pants and get moving!"

Gavin gave a final pleading look to Betty, who said, "She has a point. Come on, Gavin. You've got this."

"I guess you're right," he replied. He turned to Annie and Geoff who were now smiling. This was their chance. "Come on, Geoff," he said. "Let's join the other knights."

Geoff gave Annie's hand another squeeze and started walking with Gavin to the other side of the hall where everyone else had congregated to give the visitors privacy.

"Gavin and Geoff?" Betty called before they reached the door at the end of the hall. Her voice sounded kind of strange and Annie could have sworn she had tears in her eyes. "Take care of each other, okay?"

Gavin put his arm around Geoff and smiled. Geoff gave the thumbs up in his heavy leather glove. Annie choked back another sob, suddenly worried that she would never see them again. Then the two men turned around and walked through the doorway to join the other knights.

When the women were alone once again, Annie and Mary Kay rounded on Betty, who was carrying the grimoire. "So," said Annie. "What spells did you find?"

Betty held up her hands. She looked like she was about to cry, and not just because they just sent their friends off to battle. "There really aren't any. It's all 'to cure boils' and 'to turn your lover's mistress ugly' and stupid shit like that. The only spell in this book that seems to be of any use at all is the one we used to get here, 'To Confront Thee Adversairie.'" She paused. "And there's also this one —" Betty flipped forward two pages to the back of the page with the sigils. "'To Returne Home.' I suppose that will be useful when we're all done here and need to get back to Kalamazoo." She looked up at Mary Kay and smiled. "But it doesn't look like it will be any use to us in battle."

"Maybe we should just use the damn spell and call it a day," said Mary Kay with a shrug.

"No!" exclaimed Annie. "Not after we just watched Geoff and Gavin don shoddy armor and walk out those doors to get themselves impaled on spears and trampled by horses! We have to *do* something, preferably *before* any of the impaling and trampling happens!"

"Annie's right," Betty said. "But what do we do?"

"I don't know." Tears welled up in Annie's eyes again, but this time they weren't tears of sadness. They were tears of frustration, she realized, and anger. She couldn't believe she had led Geoff into this mess. He only wanted to network at the conference, maybe take her out on a date. Now he was fighting for his life in some medieval battle he might never return from, and it was all Annie's fault. And Marshall's fault, Annie thought bitterly. But Marshall was gone now. Annie would take the full blame for bringing her friends into this predicament, and the full responsibility for saving them.

"Guinevere," she said, and then took off at a run down the length of the hall toward the opposite door, her Doc Martens thudding ominously on the stone floor. Betty and Mary Kay took off after her.

The three of them emerged outside and Annie beelined for a small stone structure that had smoke coming through the chimney — she hoped it was the kitchen. Once inside, she knew she had guessed right. A cauldron was set up over a fire on the far wall, and Guinevere was standing over it adding dried herbs to a steaming liquid. She turned around and smiled. "Annie," she said. "Are you ready to begin? I've already begun concocting a healing potion. I will prepare some poultices next. But you — you will need to find a high ground from which to cast your combative spells."

"That's the problem," Annie said, cutting right to the chase. "We don't know any combative spells. We don't even know where we can learn any." She held up the grimoire. "All we have is this single book full of useless spells that govern mundane sixteenth-century problems, plus the spell that brought us here. We don't have any powers that will be useful against Mordred and his army."

Guinevere frowned. "That is not what Merlin told us," she whispered. "He seemed very certain — I spoke with him myself. He assured me that the people coming to avenge my Arthur's memory would be very powerful. He specifically mentioned that the group would consist of men bearing swords as well as women wielding powerful magic they did not understand..." Her blue eyes brightened up just a bit. "Is it possible that you just don't understand? That you really do have the magic, but you do not know it?"

Annie nodded swiftly. "Yes, that's entirely possible, but it won't do us any good if we don't understand it."

"Hmm, that may be."

"Do you have any manuscripts or scrolls or something?" Betty asked. "Maybe if you have a magic book or two, we can glance through them and get some ideas."

"Of course!" replied Guinevere. "You are very lucky — this particular fortress is home to Arthur's library. Follow me. I will take you there."

Guinevere left the cauldron and went outside with the other three women jogging behind her. She brought them back into the main building through yet another door that led into a room that contained nothing but books. The walls were lined with shelves and shelves of scrolls and codices. Mary Kay and Betty looked like they just stumbled into heaven. Annie turned quickly on Guinevere and asked, "Which books contain spells?"

"They all do," said Guinevere, beaming. "This was Arthur's secret collection. It is the largest library of magic in the world."

| 19 |

The Quest for Merlin

"The largest library of magic in the world?" Mary Kay raged. "Could this *be* any less helpful?" No one was around to answer her rhetorical question — Guinevere had already left them to return to the kitchen and her healing magic.

"Maybe we'll get lucky and find something useful in the first book," said Betty, though she didn't sound like she believed herself. She seemed half-hearted as she made her way over to a shelf and pulled out a codex at random.

"No," Annie said, still rooted to the spot near the doorway where she had halted when she first caught sight of the library. "We can't waste time leafing around in an endless library. I know what we need. We need Merlin."

"Merlin?" Betty asked.

Annie nodded. "We can find him. He can't be far from here. We can ask one of the servants. Come on — let's go."

"Are you sure?" Betty seemed reluctant to put down the book she was holding.

"As sure as I am of anything. You said it yourself, last night. We're here because of Merlin's spell. Basically, we're in the midst of one giant Merlin spell now." Annie laughed. To her own ears, she sounded a little maniacal, but she kept going. "It seems obvious now that I say it out loud. As long as we're here, Merlin is the answer to everything."

"She's right," said Mary Kay after a minute. Her voice was low and serious. She was terrified. "Let's go, Betty. The sooner we find Merlin, the sooner we can get out of this mess."

Betty looked through the book in her hands one more time, determined it was useless, and re-shelved it before following the others out of the library into the cool, crisp air. The sun was almost up now. They were running out of time.

It was not difficult to find where Merlin lived. Every servant lingering in the hall that morning was eager to point Annie and the others in the right direction. Merlin occupied a hut just inside the nearest forest, only about a mile's walk from the fort. Mary Kay could have made the trek in heels.

The women were in good spirits when a tiny hovel came into view in just the place where they were told it would be. "Here it is!" Betty exclaimed.

"Woohoo!" Annie said, throwing up her floppy hat in celebration.

"We made it!" said Betty. "Merlin is the answer to our prayers!"

"I don't know," said Mary Kay, suddenly stopping when they were just fifty yards from Merlin's hut.

"Oh, what is it now?" asked Betty, impatiently. "You've been such a Debbie Downer this whole trip —"

"There's no smoke coming from the chimney," Mary Kay interrupted.

"Oh." Betty and Annie both stopped in their tracks.

"I think we should go ahead anyway and check, just to be sure," said Annie. "Maybe he just doesn't have a fire going now, since it's day." Annie started forward slowly and Betty followed her, just as slowly.

"You guys go on ahead," said Mary Kay. "I'm going to sit here and rest a minute. These sixth-century shoes are killing me."

Only Annie turned around. "All right," she said. "We'll be back in a bit."

Annie and Betty approached the door, and Betty knocked. After a moment, a young girl who couldn't have been more than a teenager opened the door. "My apologies if you are here to see Lord Merlin, my ladies," she said, keeping your eyes low. "But he is out on his travels, and I beg that you excuse him. You see, Lord Merlin is always traveling in order to study the ways of the world. He is not available at the moment."

"Where the hell has he gone?" Betty practically roared.

"Tell me what you know," Annie said to the girl seriously.

"I know he tended the wounds of the lord Mordred not three days ago, but Mordred escaped during the night and that left my lord Merlin much distressed. He told me to tell any visitors who might call that he went to the future, though I don't know quite what that means."

Annie thought she had an idea. Betty, on the other hand, pushed her way past the girl. "Can I have a look at his books? He must have fighting spells in here somewhere."

"I'm going to check on Mary Kay," Annie said. She wasn't sure Betty heard her, but she turned around anyway, not wanting to be in Betty's way while she tore through Merlin's spellbooks.

Mary Kay had only been sitting on the rock for a couple of minutes when Annie returned. She had just lit a cigarette when she saw Annie approaching from the direction of the hut, alone.

"Merlin not home?" she asked, blowing out smoke.

Annie shook her head and sat down on the rock beside Mary Kay. Mary Kay held out the box of cigarettes and offered one to Annie.

"No, thank you," said Annie.

"Good choice. These are disgusting. I can't remember the last time I smoked one sober, but it wasn't a good idea then, and it isn't now." Mary Kay continued smoking the cigarette anyway.

"I'm sorry, Mary Kay," Annie said after a moment. "I know it's an extreme understatement to say this whole thing must be really stressful to you, but I promise I'll get us home."

"You do?" Mary Kay asked. She turned toward Annie, and Annie noticed for the first time that there were tears in her eyes. Underneath the stark hairstyle and the makeup of the day before and the stone countenance of a youngish woman professor whose professional dealings were normally with men of a different generation, she was a scared little girl who didn't know what was going to happen next. Underneath, she was Annie, just out of college and fresh from a breakup, scared to death of starting her new life in grad school.

Annie nodded. "I do. I promise as hard as I can." Now Annie was crying, and Mary Kay's tears started flowing freely, streaking mascara down her face.

"Can I be frank, Annie?" she asked, taking another puff of her cigarette and making a face. "I'm terrified. I'm effing scared to death I'm never going to see Bob and the kids ever again. And *that* is the worst feeling I could ever imagine having."

She reached into her bag and pulled out her phone to show Annie and sniffled. "Sometimes I just get out my phone to look at pictures of my children. Here's Michael." Annie leaned in to see a picture of a beautiful blond toddler smiling at the camera while holding up a basket filled with Easter candy. Mary Kay swiped to a picture of two older boys with dark hair fighting with foam swords. "This is Stephen and Patrick." Now she was sobbing. "I miss them so much."

"Wait," said Annie.

Mary Kay looked up mid-swipe. (The next photo showed all three boys posed on the couch, each looking more — and then less — like Mary Kay.) "What is it?" Mary Kay snapped.

"Your phone works?" Annie asked.

Mary Kay sniffled again and turned off the screen. "Of course it does. I wouldn't expect time travel to drain the battery."

"No," said Annie, "that's not what I mean. Turn the screen back on."

Mary Kay pushed the button on the side of her phone and beamed down at the children, but Annie looked past them. Her eyes went to the top of the screen and the three little bars in the upper right hand corner. She pointed them out. "Look — there's bars," she said. "You have signal."

Mary Kay stared down at her phone. "Huh," she said. "So I do."

Mary Kay's eyes lit up briefly, and Annie knew she was coming to the same realization Annie had reached a moment ago, that they could call…someone. Annie reached into her bag for her own phone and frantically started dialing.

"Who are you calling?" asked Mary Kay.

"Murray!" Annie exclaimed, gleefully holding the phone to her ear while she walked several paces into the woods.

Murray answered the phone on the second ring, as he always did. "Hello, Annie," he said. That was the way he always answered the phone, like he had just discovered Caller ID and delighted in knowing who the caller was before they got a chance to speak. And just like whenever Annie called at a scheduled time to begin a phone meeting, Murray sounded like he had been expecting her call.

"How is your conference going?" he asked. "Did the book prove helpful?"

Annie sighed. "A little too helpful," she answered. "The book contains real magic. Not only did it find its way to me at Kalamazoo, but it brought us back to sixth-century Wales to defeat Mordred and preserve Arthur's memory. That's where I'm calling from now."

"You're calling from —?"

"Sixth-century Wales. I think it's 537. I'm standing just outside of Merlin's house." Annie took a deep breath and forged on. It wouldn't help her to beat around the bush. "Your house. You weren't home, but as soon as I saw we still had cell signal here, I knew that didn't matter. I could just call you."

"Very good, Annie," said Murray. His voice sounded stronger now. Now that his secret was out. "But what do you need my help for? You seem like you understand your mission perfectly clearly."

"I understand what we have to do," Annie replied, "but I don't understand how we have to do it. Our male colleagues went into literal battle against Mordred early this morning — for all I know they could be dead now — and we're supposed to use magic to help them out, but we don't have any spells."

"What do you mean you don't have any spells?" Murray asked. "You have the grimoire, don't you?"

"Yes, but all the spells are worthless. Betty read through them this morning."

Murray laughed, for the first time in Annie's hearing. Annie didn't think he had a sense of humor. "Oh, I'm not talking about *those* spells, those silly incantations devised by sixteenth-century witches that make up most of the grimoire. I'm talking about *my* spells — in the center?"

"You mean the sigils with the inscription about Arthur's memory?" Annie asked, confused.

"No no no, that's Mordred's spell, shot with Morgan's magic, through and through. But that spell was made with my parchment, and I foresaw Mordred's betrayal and infused it with some magic of my own. You will have noticed there's a spell on either side of that parchment, disguised to look like the rest of the spells in the grimoire. Well, of course you have! You couldn't have gotten to sixth-century Wales without it!"

"'To Confront Thee Adversairie'?" Annie asked, still confused.

"There is only one real spell in that grimoire," Murray said darkly. "One real spell, and it's counterpart, that will reverse it."

Annie now realized that the other useful spell Betty flagged, "To Returne Home," appeared on the back of the second page of sigils, and must be the reversal spell. "I think I understand now," Annie said into the phone. "'To Confront Thee Adversairie' brought us here, and 'To Returne Home' will take us back."

"It is not quite as simple as that," said Murray. "The second spell doesn't just return people home — it is, like I said, a counterpart to the first. You have to confront, and defeat, your adversary first if you want the other spell to do what you want it to do."

Annie was afraid of that. She nodded and said, "I understand. But I still have the same problem I had when I called you. I don't know what to do when I confront my adversary. I don't know any combat spells. What do I do when I find Mordred?"

"I think you will find you have everything you need, Annie," Murray said.

"But I *don't*," Annie protested. She was starting to become frustrated. If Merlin had gone to the trouble of making sure she would be able to reach him from the sixth century, he should at least be able to tell her something useful. "Just because I gained some understanding doesn't mean I'm any closer to being able to defeat Mordred than I was when I first called you."

"Sure you are," Murray replied brightly. "You now know for certain that you have everything you need! Now, if you will excuse me, I have to go. My wife and I have tickets to an outdoor concert and she insists on leaving now. Goodbye, Annie, and good luck."

"But —" Annie started, but she didn't finish. Murray had already hung up.

Annie returned to the rock where Mary Kay was sitting and found Betty had joined her. "Merlin must have taken all his good spellbooks with him. Nothing in his house was of any use at all," said Betty glumly.

"Did you have any luck with your phone call to Murray?" Mary Kay asked.

"Phone call to what?" Betty asked, alarmed.

Annie ignored her. "Sort of," she said. "He's Merlin, I think. Or a reincarnation of Merlin. I've been suspecting that for a long time, now. But then when Merlin's servant said he was in the future, and when I saw you had cell signal, Mary Kay, I knew. It's been Murray all along. And he just told me everything I need to know, apparently."

"Which was?" asked Mary Kay.

Annie shrugged and sat back down on the rock. "Not a whole lot. Just that I have everything I need. Apparently."

"Wonderful!" said Betty, clapping her hands and standing up.

"Are you serious?" asked Mary Kay.

"Yes!" Betty looked giddy. "I've never been more serious about anything in my life. If Merlin says we have everything we need, then we do. Right? We're all in one big Merlin spell right now, aren't we?"

"That's the other thing," said Annie. "He said there was only one spell. To confront our adversary, and the reverse of the spell, which will bring us home after we defeat him."

"So that's what we need now," said Betty excitedly. She clapped her hands again. "Finally, we're getting somewhere!" The three of them glanced up at the sun together, noting the passage of time but not mentioning anything about it, or their male companions whose presence was heavily felt in their absence. Talking about it would do them no good. "We have the right spell," Betty said. "Now we just have to figure out how to use it."

Annie and Mary Kay looked at each other blankly while Betty pulled the grimoire back out of Annie's bag and opened to the relevant pages. "There it is," she said. "There's our spell."

"The only problem is," said Annie. "We already used it."

"Once," said Betty. "We used it once. Maybe using it again will bring us closer to our adversary."

"It's worth a shot," said Annie, shrugging.

"What else have we got to lose?" Mary Kay asked. Annie gave her hand a squeeze.

"I think we should all say it together this time," said Betty. "Maybe it will be stronger."

Annie and Mary Kay nodded and each took one of Betty's hands with their free hands.

"Ready?" Betty asked. "Go!"

| 20 |

Heroes of Legend

This time, the spell didn't open a portal. Instead, it lifted the three women full into the air and deposited them on the ramparts of Arthur's fortress. From there, they could see the battle raging below them. Frantically, Annie searched the crowd for Geoff, but it was no use. All the men looked the same in their dull armor, and they were using strategic hiding places to launch their attacks. She supposed it was a good thing if she couldn't see Geoff, then.

"Annie! You have returned!" a voice said behind her.

Annie startled and turned around. There was Guinevere, tending to the injuries of several men she did not know.

"I could really use your help." Guinevere sounded breathless. "The injured are coming in faster than I can heal them. Could one of you possibly help me with healing spells?"

"You go, Betty," Mary Kay said, pushing Betty forward. "You seem to have a greater affinity for spellwork. I'll help Annie with the adversary."

"Are you sure?" Betty asked.

"Go on," said Annie. "Those men need you more than I do right now. When I think I need to add your strength to my spell, I'll come get you."

Betty gave her an encouraging smile and joined Guinevere among the injured, looking very much in her element. Annie grabbed Mary Kay's hand and dragged her to the other side of the rampart, looking for a place where they could see the battlefield without being spotted by the enemies down below.

"What's your plan?" Mary Kay asked, trailing along.

"I don't have one," Annie admitted.

"So I guess that means we keep trying the Adversairie spell?"

Annie nodded and threw the grimoire down between her and Mary Kay. It fell open to the correct page on its own. "Merlin said we have everything we need, and this is all we have, so let's just go with it."

"Aren't you worried that if we say the spell again it'll take us right into the midst of battle?"

Annie looked up at Mary Kay and saw in her wide, brown eyes nothing but fear. This time Annie shared it. She swallowed. "That's exactly what I'm afraid of."

Mary Kay looked over her shoulder at the battle raging below them. "Do you think we should wait for Mordred to come into sight? Then maybe the spell will actually do something other than transport us."

"That's a good idea," said Annie. She joined Mary Kay up against the wall to get a better view of the battlefield. She scanned it for a moment before realizing she was looking for Geoff when she was supposed to be looking for Mordred. She couldn't see either one of them.

"There's Morgan le Fay!" Mary Kay said suddenly. She pointed and Annie turned her gaze to the left flank of the enemy army, near the entrance to a forest. Dressed in dark red robes and shimmering gold, she was impossible to miss.

Annie started to laugh. "Could she be any more conspicuous?"

"She's arrogant," said Mary Kay. "Look — that must be Mordred about twenty feet away from her."

Annie followed Mary Kay's gaze, and sure enough, there was Mordred, trying to blend in among his cavalrymen while sneaking forward in an attempt to get behind the Knights of the Round Table. "Yep, that's him!"

"So, do we do the spell?"

"I guess so."

"Even with Morgan standing right there?"

Annie looked at Mary Kay and smiled. "She's arrogant, right? I'm not worried about her. We have Merlin's spell — a completely *un*-arrogant, that is, simple, spell designed to do one thing."

"Right," said Mary Kay, instinctively clutching her tote bag. She took Annie's hand and the two of them read the spell aloud again.

In a flash of light, Annie and Mary Kay found themselves exactly where they expected to — right in the middle of the battlefield. Except they were not on the ground being trampled by horses. They were hovering above Mordred on some sort of cloud.

Morgan caught sight of them first and started hurling lightning bolts in their direction, which they were able to avoid by steering the cloud with their movement. "Witches!" Morgan shouted. Her voice was deep and otherworldly and seemed to reverberate within the very earth. "Stop them!" At her command, everyone on the field turned to look at Annie and Mary Kay, including Mordred.

"Devils begone!" Mordred shouted. "Morgan — banish them!"

"Not so fast!" Mary Kay shouted. Before Annie could stop her, Mary Kay jumped down from the cloud and began spraying Morgan's face with something she pulled out of her tote bag. Morgan gave an almighty shriek and brought her hands up to her eyes. "Get him, Annie!" Mary Kay called as she continued to spray.

Annie read the spell again, this time shouting the words. The same magical light flashed again, through which Annie could see Bedivere and Gawain arrive to relieve Mary Kay. Then she saw nothing but white.

Annie was nowhere. The cloud was gone, as were her own hands in front of her. The sounds of the battle had disappeared as well, replaced by the overwhelming sound of rushing water. Then Annie began to make out the shape of Mordred, distorted, as if through a mist. He was still on his horse, but he looked desperate, panicked. Her spell had done something to him, and he was scared. He was shouting and shouting, but Annie couldn't hear what he was saying over the rushing. This had to be the end. There was no way she would be able to perform the spell again, and if she did, there was no way she would survive it.

Just then, someone else appeared in her frame of vision along with Mordred. It was a man, dressed in the armor of Arthur and riding a horse. Annie could not identify him from behind, especially since he was wearing a helmet, but she knew there was only one person this could be.

Geoff lifted up his sword and brought it down hard on Mordred's shoulder, causing him to drop his own sword. Then, more quickly than Annie would have thought possible, he swung his sword back around and pierced the open spot between Mordred's sword-arm and his chest, knocking Mordred from his horse as he did so. The last thing Annie saw before everything went dark and quiet was the look of defeat on Mordred's face as he realized that his spell over Arthur's memory was broken.

The first thing Annie saw when she opened her eyes was Betty's face, which went from serious to elated when she saw that Annie was conscious. "She's opening her eyes!" Betty called over her shoulder.

Gavin and Guinevere appeared behind Betty, and as Annie blinked, their faces came into sharper focus. "Oh, I'm so happy you're awake," said Guinevere. "Here — drink this. It will help you heal faster."

Betty took the cup from Guinevere's hand and held it up to Annie's mouth. "Just a couple sips," she said. Then she continued in a low whisper, "I promise this is actual magic and not a weird medieval concoction of inedibles."

Annie tried to smile, but she wasn't sure if she could get her mouth to do that. Her whole body was shaking. She was able to form her lips into an O shape and allow Betty to feed her some of the potion, which gave her strength instantly.

"Where's Geoff?" Annie asked, her head suddenly clear. "Is Geoff okay?"

"Geoff is a hero!" Gavin answered from somewhere outside of Annie's range of vision. "I don't know if you were able to see, but he dealt the death-blow to Mordred. After that, Mordred's army dispersed and fled. We were only able to capture a few prisoners. But the battle is over — the spell is broken."

"Unfortunately, Geoff won't go down in history as a hero," Betty added, "since this battle didn't actually happen — it was just part of the undoing of a spell. The hero everyone will remember will be Arthur. Which is what we wanted to happen anyway, so I'd say that's okay."

"But is *Geoff* okay?" Annie asked more forcefully. "Is he hurt?"

"Oh, no," Betty answered, laughing. "He's fine, just exhausted. Guinevere had to mop him up a little but he didn't have any real injuries. Last I saw him he went in to bathe with the rest of the knights. I bet he's resting or sleeping now. You'll see him tonight at the feast."

"Feast?"

"Yeah, I know it's kind of late, but I'm told it's custom to have a feast to celebrate the ends of battles like this."

"You may bathe too, Annie," Guinevere said, reassuringly. "I have put new clothing in your room for you to change into when you're clean. Then you may rest as well. We are not expected in the hall for another couple of hours."

"Where's Mary Kay?" Annie asked. The others may have had time to recover from the battle, but Annie was just coming to. She needed to find out what happened to her friends.

"She went up for a bath a little bit ago," Betty answered. "I just finished mine." Annie took a closer look at Betty and noticed her outfit had changed. Not significantly, but the outer garment was blue instead of green and the headdress she was wearing was more of a wimple than a hat. "You can go next. And no, before you ask, you will not have to use the same bathwater."

"This was the court of a king!" Guinevere interjected. "Everyone gets her own bathwater."

"Thank you," said Annie. "But is Mary Kay okay too? I left her fighting Morgan, but she seemed to be doing all right."

Betty snorted. "She was more than all right. Can you believe she had *wasp spray* in her mom bag? Morgan didn't know what hit her! And then Gawain lifted Mary Kay onto his horse to take her out of the battle while Bedivere kidnapped Morgan, who is now in prison awaiting judgment." She held the cup to Annie's lips again, urging her to drink more. "But what about you, Annie? What did you do? One second you were up on that cloud, hovering over Mordred, and the next second you were gone, but a bright yellow star appeared just in front of Mordred's face."

"I was part of that star," Annie said, recalling the overpowering sound of rushing water and the feeling that she would cease to exist if she tried to perform the spell again. "I think I must have been holding Mordred or something, for Geoff, I guess."

Betty nodded like it was starting to make sense to her. She added, "Then after Geoff knocked down Mordred, and everyone cleared away, the star vanished too, and there you were in its place, just lying on the ground."

"At first I thought you were dead," said Gavin. "I rode right up to you. But you were breathing — just knocked out. Kei helped me put you my horse and we brought you back to the fort."

"How long ago was that?" Annie asked.

"Oh, two, three hours," said Gavin.

Betty saw the look on Annie's face and said, "Whatever that spell was, it took a lot out of you."

"Yeah, no shit," Annie said, rubbing her eyes. "Can I have the rest of that potion? I think I can hold it now."

Betty handed the cup to Annie and sat down on the bench, exhausted now that her last patient had recovered.

The rest of the evening was a blur. Annie felt refreshed after her bath, but she was still bone-weary and trying to process everything that had happened since her phone call with Murray (not to mention the fact that she now knew her PhD advisor was Merlin. She wondered how that would affect her progress to degree). Geoff and Mary Kay were both at dinner, looking radiant, and when she saw them Annie felt a surge of gratitude in her heart at having these two wonderful people come into her life.

The hall was filled with candles and a large fire lit one end of the room so that all of the finely-woven wall-hangings were visible in the flickering light. Annie regretted that her eyelids were too heavy for her properly to appreciate them. The meal at the Round Table was extravagant, but she barely tasted it. Then after the feast was dancing, but she was too tired. She declined Geoff when he put out his arm and asked if he could escort her ladyship to the dance floor. She realized she would have liked to dance with him if she weren't so tired, though, and as she drifted off to sleep on her straw mattress to the sound of Betty and Mary Kay breathing, she wondered whether they hadn't missed the dance at Kalamazoo.

The next morning, everyone got dressed in their original clothing before meeting in the great hall to say goodbye to Guinevere and the knights before they left. They all looked strange in their rumpled suits and dress shirts after Annie had gotten used to seeing them in medieval garb all weekend. Even she tugged at her sweater and jeans, seeming to notice their tightness for the first time.

"Thank you so much for all of your hospitality," Betty was saying to their hosts as they prepared to conjure the spell that would send them home. "And, of course, your help on the battlefield. We *really* couldn't have done it without you."

"Well we could not have done it without you," Bedivere replied, and he meant it sincerely. "But now you must return to your own time. Do you have everything you need?"

Annie held up the grimoire and said, "Right here. The rest of Merlin's spell is just on the other side of the parchment."

Bedivere chuckled. "That Merlin," he said. "Always subtle, but ever as clear as could be."

"But we're not all here yet," Annie said.

Gavin stretched out his neck, looking around and counting. "Why, yes we are," he said. "The three of us professors and you two grad students."

"You're forgetting Marshall," said Annie. Everyone looked at her, and Betty scowled. "He doesn't belong here. We should at least take him back."

"Marshall?" asked Kei from the other side of the room. "Do you mean that scrawny prisoner who won't stop talking?"

"That's probably him," Annie said, smiling. She never would have thought to call Marshall "scrawny," but from the perspective of the burly knight, she couldn't think of a more appropriate label.

"Good!" Kei exclaimed. "We'll be glad to be rid of him. He can be your problem — the future's problem." Then he and Gawain took off through one of the rear doors to bring Marshall back from wherever it was they kept their prisoners.

When they returned, Annie, Betty, Mary Kay, Gavin, and Geoff were all standing in a circle around the grimoire open to the final spell: "To Returne Home."

"Hey guys," Marshall said sheepishly. He was also wearing his own clothes, but by the smell of him, he hadn't bathed.

"Come on, Marshall," Annie said in as flat a tone as she could manage. "Let's go home." She took his hand and Mary Kay looked away before grabbing his other hand.

"Annie — " he started.

"You can tell me at home," Annie said. "You've taken up enough of the Knights of the Round Table's time already." She winked at Kei, who was grinning. "And besides," she continued, now looking over at Geoff, "I want to make it back to Kalamazoo in time for the dance."

"Then what are you waiting for?" Betty urged. "Say the spell!"

As they planned, Annie spoke the words of the spell alone, since "home" to her might mean something different than "home" to the others. With any luck, the portal that appeared would take them back to Valley One at the same time as they left it. When the door that sprouted in the middle of the circle looked exactly like the heavy metal fire door that led to Annie's dorm room, everyone breathed a sigh of relief.

| 21 |

The Dance

Annie found her room key at the bottom of her conference bag. Thank God she hadn't lost it. The consequences of losing the key would have been far worse than the fifty dollar fine the student volunteer at registration had warned her about. Her hand trembling, she stuck the key into the lock and turned the handle on the door and began to push it open. Early-evening sunlight was streaming through the window on the other side of the door while the hall of the Round Table was bright with morning, and for a moment Annie felt disoriented, as if she were in two places at once. Then she crossed the threshold back into Kalamazoo.

Gavin was the last to enter the dorm room, and he shut the door behind him. "It looks like the same time as when we left, two days ago," he said. "Is it?"

"Yes." Mary Kay was looking at her phone. "5:48 pm, May 13. It's still Saturday. Or Saturday again."

"We're back in Kalamazoo the exact moment we left it!" Gavin said, sounding awestruck.

"That means we didn't miss the dance," said Geoff.

At that moment Betty's phone and Mary Kay's phone both dinged. Betty pulled hers out of her pocket and grumbled, "Now I have to remember who I was supposed to meet for dinner tonight."

Mary Kay ignored her phone. "You mean you're not going to go to dinner with *us*? After all we've been through together?"

"Or me?" asked Gavin. "I drove all the way up from Indiana and you aren't even going to have dinner with me?"

Betty's face softened. "All right, just a second."

"Can I leave then? I don't think you mean to include me in your dinner plans." Marshall sounded angry and pouty, and he looked even angrier and poutier leaning up against the wall beside the door with his arms crossed. Annie was about to say "yes," but Betty spoke first.

"Not so fast," she said, shoving her phone back into her pocket. Apparently her dinner friends could wait. "I feel like you owe us an explanation." She rounded on him fast, and though Marshall was taller than Betty, Betty was formidable and Marshall seemed to cower in her presence.

"Especially Annie," Betty continued. Annie took a step backward into Geoff. "I want you to explain to Annie how you knew her book really had a spell in it, and why you used her to cast that awful spell. What did King Arthur ever do to you?"

"Nothing, I swear!" Marshall said defensively. "I'm not Mordred's great-great-great-great-grandson or anything."

"There's a relief," said Mary Kay sarcastically. Betty silenced her with a look.

"But a lot of people feel that way about Arthur," Marshall pleaded. "That he doesn't deserve all that fame, and that Mordred was misunderstood."

"Well, we just got back from 537 and can now say with confidence that none of that's true."

"*Mary Kay*," urged Betty.

"Sorry!" Mary Kay gestured for Marshall to continue.

"Just Google 'Lost Sigils of King Arthur,'" he said. "It's all over the internet. I've been following it since we first got the internet at home, when I was a kid. People have known for a long time that there was a magical plot to correct the historical memory of King Arthur, and that it had to do with the sigils. At some point, someone figured out they were hidden in some random grimoire, so I'd just been looking around for medieval grimoires. I couldn't believe it when I found the sigils in yours." He looked at Annie desperately. Annie tried to keep her face cold.

"So you're telling me," said Betty in a threatening whisper, "that this was the work of internet conspiracy theorists? So what if you found them when you were young and impressionable? I thought by now you would have known better. I thought I taught you how to read a text." She turned away, her face pure disappointment.

"I — I'm sorry," said Marshall. He looked over at Annie again, this time less desperate, more contrite. "I didn't mean to use you, Annie. I'm sorry we couldn't become friends. We were getting along pretty well the first couple days at Kalamazoo."

"Thank you, Marshall," Annie replied. "I'm sorry we can't be friends now, too. Maybe next year's Kalamazoo."

Marshall opened his mouth as if to speak but closed it. "All right. I'll go now."

"And Marshall?" Betty said before he left. "When we get back to Ann Arbor you and I can have a meeting about continuing to work with one another. Textual criticism is central to our work and we will need to decide if you are serious in that endeavor before we can continue."

Marshall nodded. "Thank you, Betty. Goodbye." He took one last look around the room at everyone and opened the door.

Only Annie waved as Marshall turned around and left the room. Everyone else was straining to see what lay beyond the threshold that Marshall had just crossed. When they saw it was indeed the dingy hallway of Valley One, they collectively exhaled. The portal had closed. Their adventure was over.

"Hey guys I was thinking," said Mary Kay, still staring at the doorway as the door slammed shut. "Do you think those discoveries we made were all part of the spell too? Like, if I turn back to Photius the passage about the warlord and the symbols wouldn't be there?"

"Maybe," said Betty, "but that would mean I didn't discover a new manuscript."

"And what the hell did *I* do all last summer?" Gavin asked. "Personally, I don't feel like finding out tonight. I say we shelve this question until tomorrow and go celebrate."

"I second that motion," said Mary Kay, pulling her phone and a flask out of her bag. "I say we pregame here, get some dinner, and then go to the dance. My late antique friends have been texting me about the dance ever since we got back to the present, and I think it's finally time to put to use this Crown Royal I've been carrying around all weekend."

"And on a related note," Geoff added, "it's finally time to show Annie what these tiny plastic cups they put in all the Valley dorm rooms are actually for." He went over to Annie's dresser and unwrapped the single plastic cup that had been sitting there untouched since Annie arrived. (She had been using the other cup to brush her teeth.)

"I hope you mean 'brush our teeth,'" said Betty through pursed lips. "Which is something we should all do right now with our fingers and Annie's toothpaste, now that I think of it. Is that okay with you, Annie?"

"Sure," said Annie. "But after we brush our teeth, I wouldn't say no to some of that Crown Royal."

"Yeah, Annie!" Mary Kay poured out a shot into the cup while Annie went to find her toothpaste.

After they freshened up and celebrated their victory over Mordred and the internet conspiracy theorists with shots of Mary Kay's whiskey taken from a single plastic cup, the five adventurers ate an unassuming dinner at the Valley Dining Hall. After dinner, they retreated to the porch outside of the first entrance to Valley Three with Geoff's water bottle full of Jameson and two six-packs of craft beer from Chicagoland that Gavin had in his trunk for this very occasion. A few minutes before ten, Annie stood up and said, "Okay, who's going to the dance?"

Geoff stood up and replied, "You know I am. We're still going together, right?"

"Yeah, we can go together," said Annie, smiling. "But what about the rest of you?"

"I'm going," said Mary Kay, picking up her tote bag and brushing herself off.

Betty shook her head. "My friends are supposed to be meeting at the Radisson for a nightcap before bed. I really should see them."

"What? You're not going to the dance?" asked Gavin.

"Betty never does anything fun," Mary Kay explained. "She doesn't stay in the Valleys, doesn't go to the night receptions, hasn't been to the dance since *I* was in grad school…"

"Come on, Betty," Gavin pleaded. "Will you do the honor of going to the dance with me? Together?"

Betty pursed her lips, trying hard not to smile, but that didn't last long.

"All right," she sighed, taking Gavin's hand. "Let's go."

Annie completely forgot about the three other dresses Gina had packed her specifically for the dance. She was still wearing the jeans, boots, and orange sweater that had taken her to the past and back, and never gave her appearance a second thought. Her hair was coarse and wavy after being washed without shampoo, and she wasn't wearing any makeup. Mary Kay had somehow managed to get her hair back into a decent French twist after her medieval bath, and of course had a whole case of makeup in her mom-bag that she had reapplied in Annie's dorm room before dinner. Betty's short hair was sticking up at odd angles, and Gavin's button-down shirt was wrinkled and the bottoms of his pants had grass stains from their first trek through sixth-century Wales. Annie was in awe of Geoff who looked as he always did, comfortable. He clapped his hands together and led the way up the hill to the Kalamazoo dance.

When they arrived, Annie noticed that no one there really looked any worse than they did. Some people had gotten dressed up, but most were still wearing their suits or sweaters or whatever they had on all day for the conference. Some looked like they tried to dress up but didn't do it very often and went a little overboard. Annie laughed with relief as she walked through the door with her motley group of avengers. They fit right in. Annie had been worried for so long about fitting in in academia, at Kalamazoo, when she had been a perfect fit all along.

Once inside the dark room, everyone dispersed. Gavin seemed eager to lead Betty onto the dance floor. Mary Kay spotted her friends by the bar and told Annie she would come back for them in a little bit after she caught up with Andrew and Dave. Annie was about to head for the dance floor as well — "Club Can't Handle Me" was playing — but Geoff stopped her. "Annie, there's something I want to say first, before we start dancing," he said.

He looked serious, so Annie followed him to the side of the room away from the speakers where she could hear him talk.

"What's up?" Annie asked, smiling and swinging Geoff's hand along to the music.

Geoff took a deep breath. "Annie," he said, "before we go out there and dance and whatever else that might happen, I just want you to know that I really *like* you like you."

"You do." Annie was still smiling but stopped dancing. She wasn't ready for a guy to tell her he liked her. She wasn't ready to like someone back yet.

"Yeah, I do. But I don't just mean I'm romantically interested. I mean, I am, but I want to make sure you know that I like you inside, as a person," Geoff continued. "I respect you. I want to tell you now, before we start dancing, that if the dancing leads to anything romantic I don't want this to just be another conference hookup."

"Ew!" Annie exclaimed, taken aback. "What's a conference hookup?"

Geoff raised both of his eyebrows. "You seriously don't know? Look around — it's what a bunch of people in this room are doing right now. People come to Kalamazoo and act like kids at summer camp. Mostly it's just single people hooking up, but I bet there's some cheating going on as well. Anyway — all I'm saying is — if we hook up, I don't want it to be like that."

"I would never do something like that," said Annie, a little offended. She had only thought about dancing and nothing more. "Who do you know that even does that?"

Geoff shrugged. "Betty and Gavin? They've been making eyes at each other all weekend. Look — now they're all over each other. No don't look!" he added when Annie turned to the dance floor where the two older professors were holding on to each other, dancing to the Ed Sheeran song as if it were their wedding dance.

"You're wrong, Geoff." Mary Kay was back just like she had promised. "They really care about each other, too. You would have had no way of knowing this because you just met them, but Betty and Gavin are actually old exes. They go back a really long time. They just never wanted to figure out what they meant to each other and how to work the whole long-distance thing. Maybe now that Betty's in Michigan instead of Maryland..." She trailed off, smiling sentimentally at her friends on the dance floor. "It is really a sweet love story."

"Okay, bad example," Geoff said sheepishly.

"Don't worry about it," said Annie. "It's probably a thing. People probably do it. But I'm not like that. I don't 'just' hook up with people."

"Whoa, what did I just walk into?"

"Sorry, Mary Kay," Annie said. But she didn't care that the older woman was listening. They time traveled together. They slept in the same bed. Mary Kay could hear how she felt about Geoff. "I like you too, Geoff," Annie said. "I'm not sure if I'm ready to do anything romantic just yet, but I have really enjoyed spending time with you at this Kalamazoo and want to keep that going. So let's just go dance, okay?"

"All right," Mary Kay started as she took a step backward into her large friend Dave who had just materialized behind her.

"Hey, watch where you're going, MK. What are you doing over here? We need to tell the DJ to play 'Electric Slide.'"

"That's my favorite part of the Kalamazoo dance," said her British friend Andrew. "Watching all these medievalists try to do the Electric Slide."

"God, *I* can't even do the Electric Slide," said Mary Kay. Annie winked at her as she grabbed onto Geoff's hand and pulled him toward the dance floor. "Have fun, you two!" Mary Kay called back. "Enjoy the dance!"

| 22 |

What Happens at Kalamazoo

Annie met Geoff outside of Valley Three the next morning to go to the book exhibit together. Annie couldn't believe it was Sunday and she still hadn't been to the book exhibit. They never actually made it to the books, though, because they ran right into Betty, Gavin, and Mary Kay standing around a table in the hallway just outside the exhibition hall.

"Hey guys! How was your night last night?" Annie asked the professors.

"Oh, it was nice!" said Betty. "Who knew the Kalamazoo dance could be so fun?" She was more smiley than usual, but nothing else would suggest anything was out of the ordinary with Betty.

"How was your night?" Mary Kay asked Annie. She was wearing jeans and a long-sleeved t-shirt and glasses, and her clean blond hair was pulled back in a ponytail. Annie and Geoff just smiled, and Mary Kay grinned back, raising her eyebrows.

"Well, I have some news to report," Betty said matter-of-factly. For a moment, Annie thought she was going to announce something about her and Gavin, but instead she said, "It turns out, I did discover a new manuscript last year. It just has nothing to do with King Arthur."

Annie had almost forgotten they were going to check if their discoveries had been part of the spell too. It turns out they were. Or at least Betty's was.

"Here — I'll show you." Betty went to the University of Michigan website on Gavin's laptop and found the story about herself. It was almost the same as the story Annie had read with Gina, except the content of the Welsh poem Betty had discovered was different.

"And I found a lot of interesting stuff on my trip to Wales last year," Gavin said, taking the laptop from Betty and opening an image file on his desktop. "No sigils here, but I definitely found some evidence of settlement, and I think a lot of small finds went with them. I'll have to study the images when I get home and get myself caught up on my own research!"

Annie started to laugh. Then she turned to Mary Kay. "What about your discoveries?" she asked.

"Oh, yeah," Mary Kay said. "I was right — none of those Arthur references I 'found' were really there. But it looks like I did have some other good ideas about Jordanes and Fortunatus and have the beginnings of a second book on my hard drive now, so there's that."

"Wow, congratulations!" Geoff said. He still looked partially in awe every time he talked to Mary Kay.

"What about Buzzfeed?" asked Annie.

"That's gone too," Mary Kay said. "And if you look at Twitter, nothing any of us Tweeted yesterday exists. The hashtag is completely gone. Like none of it ever happened."

"So this whole Kalamazoo was a bust then," said Betty, throwing up her arms.

"Yeah, a real bust," said Mary Kay. "I'm so sorry I made you drive all the way up here for nothing, Gavin." She winked at Gavin and everyone burst out laughing.

"I don't know about you, Annie, but I have never networked this well at a conference before," said Geoff.

"Well, this is my first conference," Annie said.

Mary Kay's jaw dropped.

"Your first?" said Gavin. "Boy, you must have learned a lot in a short time — by the time I met you, you seemed like an old pro."

"She's a natural," said Betty, clapping her hand on Annie's back. "Okay, so the social aspect of the conference wasn't a bust, but the whole King Arthur thing really was — we have to agree on that."

"No we don't," said Mary Kay.

"What do you mean?" asked Betty.

"I mean, twenty-four hours ago — or, twenty-four present-day hours and forty-odd past hours ago — we were all patting ourselves on the back for how good at collaborating we all were. We just solved a humongous mystery about King Arthur and we did it by working together across disciplines. But then it turned out we were all being manipulated by some Merlin spell, so none of that actually happened. But that doesn't mean it couldn't happen, or shouldn't happen. That doesn't mean we shouldn't collaborate across disciplines."

"So what you're saying is," said Betty, "you want us to pitch a session on collaborative methods of Arthurian studies?"

"Precisely."

"Sorry, MK, you're on your own for this one. I've already agreed to chair a panel for next year."

"So have I," said Gavin sadly.

"I can co-chair the session with you," Annie found herself saying.

"Great!" Mary Kay replied enthusiastically. "If you want, I'll write up the proposal — it's due in a couple weeks. Then we can both read submissions." She looked pointedly at Betty and Gavin as if to say "You had better submit something." "It could be something as simple as, 'Interdisciplinary Approaches to Arthurian Britain.'"

"Or even: 'Interdisciplinary Approaches to Thwarting Internet Conspiracy Theorists,'" said Geoff.

"Even better," said Mary Kay, "Misinformation and problematic medievalism is rampant on the internet, as we all kind of learned the hard way this weekend, but online communication can also be a tool to combat it. How does that sound to you, Annie?"

"It sounds great," Annie exclaimed.

"Is it too late to change my mind?" asked Betty.

"Of course not," Annie answered. "I would love to keep working with you two."

"I'm looking forward to working some more with you, too, Annie." Mary Kay smiled and reached one arm out for a hug, and Annie leaned in. "It's been so nice spending time with you this weekend. I look forward to meeting again at Kalamazoo next year. I have to get on the road now, though."

"Why so soon?" Annie asked. It was only nine-thirty in the morning.

"I have a long drive ahead of me, and I need to make it home in time for dinner. It's Mother's Day, and my husband and sons always prepare a special Mother's Day dinner for me on the day I get home from Kalamazoo. It's one of my favorite family traditions. After a weekend like this, I miss them more than ever."

Annie nodded and Betty stepped forward and embraced Mary Kay. "I bet you do," she said softly. "Go home — tell Bob I say hi. I promise we'll have more time to catch up next year."

"You say that every year," Mary Kay said, picking up her tote bag and rolly suitcase.

"This time I mean it. Safe travels, Mary Kay."

"Goodbye."

Betty and Gavin left a few minutes later, ostensibly to catch up with more of Betty's friends she had missed the day before. Then Annie and Geoff were left alone with the books.

They wandered around in the exhibit for a little while, vaguely looking at titles, but Annie realized she wasn't interested in looking at the books. That was odd for her, who normally loved books. Something that she had on her mind, which had been there since she woke up that morning, was interfering with her concentration.

She stopped suddenly when they got to the far end of the book exhibit and put her hand on Geoff's arm. "Geoff?" she asked

Geoff turned, and when he saw the look on Annie's face, his face fell, like he knew what was coming. They had so much fun at the dance together, but Annie still wasn't interested in dating him.

"Geoff, I want to thank you so much for what you did for me this weekend," Annie said earnestly, looking right into Geoff's sincere brown eyes that had only ever looked at her with kindness. "You will never know how much it means. I told you that I had a long-term boyfriend in college, and that I haven't dated anyone at all in the three years after college, but you will never understand how hard it was for me to get to a point where I could even think about becoming close with someone else after that. But you helped me. You got to know me, and made me feel comfortable, and made me feel good about myself, and never feel trapped, and —"

She started to cry. When she imagined having this conversation with Geoff as they wandered through the books, it didn't include crying. Perhaps her tears indicated how much she truly did care about Geoff. She hoped he would understand. "Thank you, Geoff. Thank you for helping me share myself with other people."

Geoff put out his hand to stroke Annie's face. "You're welcome, Annie," he said. "I have enjoyed every minute of getting to know you and I can't tell you how happy I feel inside that you allowed me to become close to you. But why are you crying?"

"Because I don't want to go out with you, Geoff."

"Oh." Geoff put down his hand, but he didn't take his eyes off Annie's.

"I'm not ready to commit to another relationship," Annie said, sniffing. "I'm barely ready to date. And you living in Chicago makes that difficult. And —"

She stopped, but Geoff prompted her, "And what else?"

"And I don't want to lose the first true friend I made at Kalamazoo by dating him." She started to laugh and Geoff laughed a little too. "I know you're hurting now, and I'm hurting too, but I think this is the right decision for me. I think I have to ease back into this slowly, you know? And I want your friendship. I want to be your good, medievalist, Kalamazoo friend, like Betty and Mary Kay are good Kalamazoo friends. I don't want to date you and then eventually dump you and never speak to you again."

"So you're playing the long game," Geoff said after a moment.

"I think," Annie said slowly, "if you want a relationship to unfold over a series of Kalamazoos, like Brigadoon, you have to play the long game."

"Fair enough," Geoff said. There were now tears in his eyes.

"But I hope you'll play the long game with me, Geoff. I hope I'll see you at Kalamazoo next year. And I hope you'll submit a paper to mine and Mary Kay's session."

"Of course I will."

"And, who knows? Maybe if we're both still single this time next year we can take each other to the dance again. That was fun, wasn't it?"

"It was," Geoff agreed. "But you don't really believe what you're saying right now, about next year, do you?"

"I don't know what things will be like next year, honestly." Annie sighed. "But I do know how I feel now and what I want to do next, and this is as certain as I've felt about something in a long time. I have to go with my gut on this one, okay?"

"Okay. Thanks for being honest with me. You're a true friend." Geoff smiled weakly, and Annie smiled back. "I'll see you next year."

"See you next year!"

After bidding goodbye to Geoff, Annie had nowhere to go but home. But she was ready to go home. Brushing the remaining tears out of her eyes, she speed-walked out of the book room and all the way up the hill to Valley One where she packed up her bag, tossing the now-useless grimoire on top, returned her $50 key at the registration desk, and got into her car.

Annie had her phone out before she even left Western Michigan's campus. She still had one lingering question about the events of the weekend and hoped that one phone call would give her the answers she needed.

"Hello, Annie," Murray's quiet voice said over the phone. "How was your Kalamazoo?"

"We did it, Murray," she said a little weakly. "We actually did it. We defeated Mordred, and Morgan le Fay, and restored the memory of King Arthur."

"Very good, Annie. I knew you could do it. And you had help from some top-notch scholars, too. I think this Kalamazoo was good for you." Murray's voice sounded proud.

"But I also had help from you," Annie said. She decided to be frank. "You're Merlin. So what does that mean for my dissertation? Are you really a historian, or —?"

Murray chuckled. This was the second time Annie heard him laugh. "Or do I just remember the sixth century because I lived through it? No. You have nothing to fear about that. I am not a time traveler. That is a distinction that only one of us holds."

"Then how are you Merlin?"

"I have the soul of Merlin. The soul of Merlin has reappeared many times throughout the ages. Perhaps Merlin in the sixth century is able to use my experience of the twenty-first, or the experiences of the other people whose persons he has inhabited. But I am still Murray Penge. I am still a historian by training and my research skills and my historical insight are my own. I have no competitive edge for being Merlin, if that's what you were wondering."

Annie felt oddly relieved. At first she thought, how cool would it be to have Merlin as her advisor? But she was grateful she still had Murray. "Thanks Murray. You know what? I think I'm ready to begin working on my dissertation."

"I know you are. How about we meet on Friday at two and you can show me what you have so far."

Annie smiled. "Sounds like a plan. I'll see you then."

Still smiling, she ended the phone call, but she didn't put down the phone. She was now on the highway where she would be for the next ninety minutes, and she had the sudden inspiration to call Gina. Annie briefly wondered whether Gina would be awake — she tended to sleep late on Sunday mornings — but then decided that if she didn't call now, the feeling might disappear and she might never get a chance to talk to Gina about this very important matter. This matter that suddenly seemed more important than the issue of her advisor.

"Hello, Annie?" Gina answered on the second ring, just like Murray. She had been awake.

"Hey Gina," Annie said, trying to sound casual. "I'm on my way home from the conference. Should be there in about an hour and a half."

"So what do you have to tell me that's so urgent it can't wait an hour and a half?" Gina asked suspiciously. How was it she could tell what Annie was thinking?

"Oh, I just had a thought, and wanted to ask you before I forgot."

"Go on," said Gina.

"I was wondering if tonight you wanted to help me make an online dating profile?"

"You're shitting me, right?"

"No, I — well I don't really know any other ways to meet guys, outside of conferences."

"You *met* someone at the *conference?*"

Annie knew Gina could sense her smile over the phone. "Yes, but... he's just going to be a friend," she said, not wanting to go into details. "But he got me thinking. I think I'm ready to date again. Like really date. Meet people. Go to coffee. Try to find someone who compliments me, who I like being around. Kind of like you and Ed."

"Well sure!" Gina exclaimed. "Online dating worked for Ed and I. I'm sure you'll at least have some success. I'd be happy to help you make a profile. But are you sure you're ready?"

The sun moved out from behind a cloud and Annie put on her sunglasses. "After Kalamazoo," she said, "I feel like I'm ready for anything."

* * *

CPSIA information can be obtained
at www.ICGtesting.com
Printed in the USA
BVHW041142110521
607045BV00014B/214